THE BOOK OF
THE LAST
WORD

JESI BENDER

Whisk(e)y Tit
NYC & VT

Published in the United States by Whisk(e)y Tit: www.whiskeytit.com. If you wish to use or reproduce all or part of this book for any means, please let the author and publisher know. You're pretty much required to, legally.

ISBN: 978-1-7329596-1-3

Library of Congress Control Number: 2018915333

First Whisk(e)y Tit paperback edition.

Cover art by Katrina Haffner.

To Barton D. Seager – A man of limitless support and an inimitable storyteller who remains a constant source of inspiration

"Dying words have a better than usual chance to survive.
There are reasons, reasons rooted very deep in human nature,
why men pay particular attention to them and preserve them.   ...
Peoples far distant in time, place and customs have joined
in the feeling that the utterance
which is never to be followed by any other
is by that very fact significant. ...
Death can make even triviality momentous, and delirium oracular.
Last words have an aura about them, if not a halo."

– from LeComte's *Dictionary of Last Words*

Patriarchy is the power of the fathers:
a familial, social, ideological, political system in which men
– by force, direct pressure, or through ritual, traditions,
laws and language, customs, etiquette, education,
and the division of labor,
determine what part women shall or shall not play,
and in which the female is subsumed under the male…
The power of the fathers has been difficult to grasp
because it permeates everything,
even the language in which we try to describe it.
– Adrienne Rich

PROLOGUE

In the beginning, there was nothing but me. In the end, it will be the same.

This is a story, at its essence, about two people. Two people who define 'good' in very different ways. And people tend to focus on the differences, instead of seeing the similarities. But, in order to understand this story, try thinking of all people as one entity, instead of separating them into categories. As one body of many, many cells. Humanity, I suppose. There, the line between good and evil will fall away because the body subsumes both—there is no dichotomy between the two (inside One).

But if people are all cells of one larger body, than there must invariably be cancer cells, sleeper cells, gnawing away at existence. Then, the dichotomy is restored! (right?)

If so, for what purpose?

What does this speak of free will?

Two, one, zero.

Some cells believe they are improving something so vast they need symbols in order to conceptualize it. Some cells see change as the only salvation, death as the only way to life. One might call them cancer. Others 'evil'. Sometimes they simply don't realize how destructive they've been. When Arthur and Chimera came to know each other, they didn't know which category the other fit into. They didn't know where they themselves fit in.

It all comes down to conscious movement. Constant improvement for a cell's capacity—that reworking of a million wrong choices. This life in constant repair.

Some cells don't have a choice. Some cells exist to serve some minor purpose and then die, a-pop!-tosis. They flake off into infinity, tiny wisps of un-existence, snowflakes dissipating into the black. Chimera Aoki was an inconsequential snowflake, only a cell on the tongue of humanity. She faded from a brilliant, pulsating red to a deep, rotting grey as she floated off the very tip.

Cells in the mouth, by the way, are the quickest at regeneration; they are the purgatorial still-borns, the teenage suicides, and the "only the good die young" accidents.

So Chimera Aoki's energy was sitting atop all of existence's tongue, one apart and a part of One, a peacefully ignorant decomposition, when she first met the siblings Numen-Noyes and their father

Arthur. It would only be three months later when consequence, fate, whatever you'd like to call it, swept her grey, bloated corpse-like cell into infinity. When she died, the body was in Elizabeth, New Jersey.

Want to know what death feels like?

A tidal wave of coagulated mint jelly, the forceful bristles of a candy-apple red, and an indescribable feeling of floating and melting at the same time.

1.

ISADORA DUNCAN SAID, "ADIEU, MES AMIS. JE VAIS A LA GLOIRE!"

There were a lot *Amen*s and a few *Hallelujah*s. She found many *Thy Kingdom come, Thy will be done*s. *Jesus*es, *Mary*s. She decided to spare her audience the *Help me*s—of which there are quite a few. *I am hot*s. *I am cold*s. The affirmatives and negatives. The references to sleep.

Deaths that have been documented seem to fall into three categories: those that were able to wither away in the presence of loved ones, those that have been immortalized in lore, and the suicides that have documented their last steps away from this world. Of course there are many of those who passed without documentation; they remain painfully mute, like a phantom limb.

All truth? No, there was a large mythology there. But perhaps the words that have been placed in their mouths speak more to the meaning of their lives than what their actual lives did.

I wish I could quote them in their original tongue. Some just said goodbye.

***

Leaving the city with a horrible twinge of sorrow pitted deep in her abdomen, Chimera leaned forward to watch the images fleeting by in between the smudged fingerprints and face-marks on the bus window. As they passed through lower Manhattan, the glowing yellow signs covered the bodies below with a perverse sunlight. Those bodies lit their cigarettes and arched their backs against their buildings. They moved inside as a shadow framed in light. Further back, the black loomed, running along side the Greyhound in clumsy, tumbling waves down the sidewalk, and, for a moment, she thought about the L underneath everyone moving back to Brooklyn. She was reminded of the two siblings and what she had found in the middle of Arthur's bed. The enamel of her teeth flashed as she bit her lip and allowed the tears to roll down her face like wind-whipped raindrops against the window.

Where am I going? Chimera thought, looking down at her bloody hands. Her knuckles were swollen and the inside of the bus smelled of iron and salt. It smelled like New Jersey, a low-hanging cloud. It was raining heavily outside.

She looked down at the papers in her hands, the manuscript smudged along the sides. She had finished writing her first manuscript—a book of deathbed decrees. A book of last words. If this book had a soundtrack, it would be silence with an almost muted muttering—a woman speaking intangibly but continually and a woman's voice nonetheless. It would be as rhythmic and arrhythmic as a human voice, a lopsided beat with the octave of estrogen; it would have an undeniably maternal cadence. Beside her, both children sat slumped over on top of themselves in slumber. The three of them were moving away from that bed, away from Arthur, though Chimera felt something unseen tugging at her to go back. There was a familiarity there; a routine, a touch, and its smells. The smells were different here—she was seated close to the bathroom.

You're never here, she complained to herself. *Here. Oh, Arthur.*

When Chimera was young, she would get horribly homesick. She still carries it with her as an adult. Whenever she is too far away—not from a place necessarily but from people. Right now, one person. Arthur. As she leaned back into the seat, she thought about how she was now an entire world away from him—her mind crossed the distance between them and a sick, hollow feeling grew inside but she couldn't tell if it originated from her stomach or her heart.

It made her feel this compulsion to scream until the bus driver stopped right there, in the middle of the Holland Tunnel, and stopped the cars, trucks and buses full of people behind them so she could run out. So she could go back and find what was missing (she still didn't understand everything that had happened). So she could ask him *Why?*

But her lip just bled, and her heart got so big that it choked. The bus rattled on towards reality with a load full of strangers, its engine humming to the beat of the muffled sobs, so wet and heavy that they floated through the air, filling the hollow, darkened body with the sorrow of some poor, little girl, using her hair to soak up the tears from the very last seat by the mini-bathroom. No one looked back, no one chose to hear, and no one cared that she was not crying for herself, or for him. No one cared about the siblings and what she found in Arthur's bed. Leaning over, she hugged the boy, trying to absorb his pain. Behind them, a man wheezed as he tried to shove his immense body into the opening of the bathroom and she cried.

Everything seemed so pathetic in New Jersey.

2.

HUNTER THOMPSON WROTE – *RELAX – THIS WON'T HURT*

Arthur Noyes was seated in his sanctuary. It was quiet and he was alone. He was talking to himselves.

From the very beginning, the problem has been that people see too much importance in themselves. The Greeks called it hubris. People saw divine and inalienable rights materialize out of ether. Look around this city!

He was thinking about men. About monuments to men. Made by men. For men. He was thinking about how pathetic men could be.

Weak.

Vain.

Little creatures.

He was thinking he could save them.

It's all bluster. How we bump into and off of each other, across the surface of this life. How we compulsively measure each movement. Each acquisition. Each conquest. Must delineate where we've been, must define. Time and lines, time and lines. Different forms of separation. We get lost in the dark with different tongues and faces and trajectories. Sometimes you just want to reach out and feel something else warm and soft and hold onto it for a moment, really feel it before you stumble on.

I have something soft and malleable in my hands. I can make it into anything I want. It beats like a foreign heart. It leaves reverberations off of the black walls of this cave, a fading glossola-la–la-lia.

Arthur's thoughts turned to the first time he met Pesach and his sister—

Before the first time I met my children, I had never held a brand-new baby. The girl wasn't an infant; she was about three. But the boy was an infant, he was closed-eyed and deep red. Almost aglow. Swaddled tightly in a blue blanket, I could tell from a distance how fragile he was and I could feel the warmth from his little body. The girl was porcelain but my son was deep red and all the more delicate. I had children in a state of purity. He was of my sister but I was the Father. No, I never was the Father; but I am the Father. It was all the more a blessing because there was no need for debasement. No part of it rooted in sin. Unlike Jews where the mothers carry their bloodline, in Christianity, it was Mary (without sin) who kept Jesus pure because G-d was his Father. And the Father was the Son. And They were Holy.

A red pulse (inside)—pulsating deep red like my heart, my heart held in my hands. Little shudders, new lungs shaping fresh noises from its crevices, and I looked down to him in my arms and I saw my hands, the size of dinner plates, engulfing his body—they were a father's hand, they were my Father's hands, I saw their color and their creases, the thick slabs for fingernails lined with dirt, the smell of the farm. I almost dropped my son when I saw his hands, when I lost my own. I felt old and powerful and lost between something concrete and ethereal. Where was I?—between a fractal of Father and Son circling onward, smaller and smaller.

Before Arthur, no one wanted these children, Pesach and his sister. No one was around to protect them. Somehow, they slipped through all the cracks. Often, the most dangerous person is someone who acts in the role of parent to a child, someone who knows something you don't, someone who is responsible for exposing you to truths because they easily can make something wrong seem very right. When you're a child, it is hard to see outside the shadow of your Father.

Arthur thought, when he came into their lives, that he saved them from the crowd. From their ugliness. From untruth. The crowd sees a burden in the body. They question whether the spirit is a part or apart of the flesh. They forget that anything can be rectified. Arthur couldn't trust what they said, their interpretations. He couldn't trust anyone else to teach his children the right way. He had only learned it himself through some type of divine intervention. And sometimes it felt like Arthur was the only one who knew that a few simple adjustments, the flesh could become a conduit for good rather than an instrument for evil.

"For in Him dwells all the fullness of deity in bodily form."

He was thinking he could save them all from their sadnesses.

Arthur's mouth was a pomegranate, thick and red, spreading across his skin, somewhere between hate and mirth. The seeds of his teeth punctured the space between and his lips parted so the juices of his mouth ran forth, as thoughts stained the air like blood from a fruit. Of these thoughts, these spoken—there was always a silence. There was decency to think of. The face you show in front of the crowd. It was protection as much for his children as for himself. So he sat there in silence, smiling pure contempt through the deep purple of his thick, fleshy lips.

Great men live outside the laws of man, those frozen lips told him. *You are a great man. Who could make great men. For all men.*

Some people are special. More special than others. Though rare, no one would dispute that they exist. They see things in ways different from everyone else. They can understand things we read everyday but never connect. Arthur read everything. This house was covered in words and Arthur spent all his time connecting the infinite into something finite.

Christ. Chrisssssssssst. Ka-rice-sssssssssssssssst.

Father used to say, "You're giving me attitude with those s's. Just say Yes// (blunt) when I tell you to do somethin'".

The room was half-lit and cold when those lips told him that he knew how to save them. His children. Sun spilt from the sole window and it disseminated upon the flakes of dust that swam in the cool spaces between. His throat worked, swallowing hard against the silence, as the still mouth spoke without any censoring speech.

The scene looked like a man complacently choking, in a barren white room, sitting on an over-turned box, his left hand down the front of his pants.

Eventually, he would confess out loud to everyone the workings of G-d that he was going to implement. With only a few words, he confessed, declaring that he found the G-d in every man, he was every man—he was G-d. An auditory ejaculation with its promise of salvation hit the cold air as he became cloaked in night.

Yessssss. Oh Chrisssssst.

I have a secret, Arthur Noyes said to the black room. No one was there, but everybody already knew.

3.

WHEN ASKED BY A COP WHO HAD SHOT HIM, TUPAC SHAKUR ANSWERED WITH A SIMPLE, *"FUCK YOU."*

Anyone who has lived in a city, in any real densely populated area, inevitably has had the thought that there are too many people in this world. Billions. There are Billions of people in this world. Moving and working. Writhing. Chimera had been living with Delores at 6 Clinton Street, Apartment 3, just on the other side of the Williamsburg Bridge in Manhattan, for approximately three years when she first met Arthur. Magic three—a dark trinity. This tiny street, a handful of blocks (3) between Houston and Delancey, at some point in time had housed quite a few famous artists.

At that specific moment, among others, it housed two lovers having a conversation about movement and stasis—too inside the magic to actually see it around them. Chimera was in the middle of researching for her book and biographies littered the floor around their mattress.

"We could move to California and sit on the beach all day long. And relax. And write. [she pointed down] Or paint. [she pointed up] We must know someone who's out there already." It didn't help that it was December in New York.

"No offense but fuck LA." Delores said without turning around.

"What—why?"

Delores shrugged. "I'm not impressed." Flippantly.

"But I thought you said you've never been there."

"I live in New York," she said, looking up, sounding annoyed. For no reason, she kicked a solitary biography across the floor. "So I've been everywhere."

She paused and then hunched over with her hands in front of her face. She whispered in a quiet sneer, a crinkled nose and fingers dancing off her thumbs, "Pre*tend*, pre*tend*, pre*tend*."

Such distain, like it was a bad thing. Like they weren't all doing the same thing.

"Alright, never mind. Let's just stay right here and live in a shithole with no money and shitty jobs and eat dollar dumplings for the rest of our lives." The words came without agitation. More sulky. Chimera felt lost. They had been falling out of love for a while now.

"Good." Delores turned away and moved towards the bathroom, their only other room. "Sounds great." The words came without agitation as well. The door closed behind her.

Sitting on the bed, Chimera looked at the closed door and thought –

I have touched her brown face;
I have felt those scars.
I have been there—
I have been to every one.
I have been in this same room
for three years.
Nothing has changed
except I remove the dust.
Periodically, I tape the pictures back up
that fall to the floor.
I am both 25 and 28; I am both now and then.
The same cars still spill off
the Williamsburg Bridge onto
the street outside and the old Mexican
ladies push around their carts.
On Friday nights, I watch the Orthodox
men help their fathers to shul
and Saturday mornings I push through

the same faces lined up for brunch
when I walk her dog.
Every night I go to sleep
with the same brown face,
although it is away from me,
and I breathe into a mass of black curls.

Chimera stood on realization of that final thought and moved towards the door, draping a thin coat around her shoulders as she passed.

A bleak December rain-snow covered the sky in a flimsy, white gossamer. Chimera walked underneath with her fists pushed deep into her coat pockets. She left Apartment 3 without saying goodbye. Wandering down the street, she felt her body heat dissipating. In some perverted way, it made her happy.

She moved against a current of pedestrians. The streets were full on Houston, Saturday night, and she moved through indifferent noise. The clusters of people collected snowflakes in their hair. The snowflakes did not ignore her; the black air was laced with fragments that found their way to her as well. A few settled in her eyelashes before she brushed them away.

A woman was walking a small distance ahead, heading in the same direction. She had her arm entwined within a man's and her hand rested inside his front jean pocket. Her voice was a continuous gay chirping that rose above the emissions of the impatient traffic. It filled the air and her words spread across Chimera who was watching her from behind. The woman bounced on her heels, swaying her thick thighs to a silent beat, and her round body bobbled to the rhythm of her voice. The chirping swayed with her body and flowed in its tremolo along the sidewalk. It blanketed the man looking down on her and he smiled in its warmth. Grey lips spread wide and leaked soft, grateful laughs through his teeth.

She remained seemingly unaware of the complete rapture in which she held the man. He walked blindly down the street, led solely by the comforting arm snaked around him. From his height, he looked down on her, straining his neck to the left, and never lifting his eyes. The wet night seemed to comfort her. Her brown skin glowed underneath the yellow streetlights and her cheeks burned pink. Chimera furrowed her brow and bit down hard on her thin, blue lips. She turned her head and caught her reflection in the window of a closed electronics store. Her skin glowed sickly and yellow in the mirrored image watching her from the darkness. Her eyes disappeared underneath the shadows, leaving two large empty sockets like a hollowed-out skeleton.

Turning suddenly, Chimera closed her eyes tightly against the image of her corpse and gripped her lip. The faint taste of blood began to fill her mouth. Their brown bodies melted together in the distance as she turned her eyes towards the sky to watch the concrete branches writhe wildly between the snowflakes in the wind.

A few moments later, she was there. The show was in a tiny basement bar owned by a fat Russian named Antov. He stood outside smoking cigarettes and shining his angry face over every paid entry. He was a stereotype, but Chimera supposed she was as well. The sign outside read 'Pravda' and of course it was a vodka bar. This was Soho but not the Soho of their forefathers. It was not a romantic relic of dilapidated artist warehouse apartments. Now no one lived here, no one they knew at least—at night, these kids crawled inland from Chinatown and Brooklyn, or, like Chimera, from underneath the austere vestiges of the brown brick behemoths dotting the east shoreline—the projects of the LES. Down the stairs and black movements were happening on stage while a monotonous beat droned, introducing her into the club, and she situated herself into a space large enough for herself and her coat.

Delores had been harping on her about being more social lately, encouraging her to go out, to find some friends and be happy.

"I have a lot of friends." Delores had said as they washed dishes together in the kitchen sink. The sink was stopped and filled with murky, brown water.

"Yes, I know." Chimera nodded, drying a plate with an old towel.

"Social interaction."

"Yes. I know what friends are for."

So Chimera was there at Pravda surrounded by people but she was there without will or much forethought. Something seemed to have guided her there and Chimera named that something Delores, though of course she was wrong.

Step 1. Order double whiskey. Drain immediately.

Step 2. Order another whiskey and a beer, trade sips between them.

(Keep beer can as decoy for contents of the flask in your purse)

The show began as an ancient dance in Technicolor. There was a ram's skull on stage held by a black girl with white-blonde hair covered in glitter. Her black veil curled right above ruby lips. A stuffed crow was affixed to the microphone stand and candles were lighted in a half-circle around the performers. Green and yellow spheres danced across the ceiling in alternating patterns. When the light caught the dust in the air, it sparked like little snowflakes lazily swimming across the room. It was very pagan—the altar and the offering. And the audience watching, holding themselves as close to 'the event' as possible without becoming a part of it (culte de l'arte, une belle massa damnata). There was the damp, dank smell of an old bar and patchouli-laced sweat. Dark, hot, everyone's hair everywhere and dramatic lines. Before the end of the second song, Chimera was kind-of drunk and couldn't tell if the person she was speaking to (shouting at) is unintelligible (I can't hear) or if they were speaking another language. {*Ah, oui, je parle un petit pois.* You're saying peas. *What?* Peas! *What?!*}

A quiet man she knows is now on stage, and nothing is perfect, but there was something magical about art released from reticent lips like a rainbow in the dark. A bizarre but electric creature moaning to the beat, and Chimera felt a sad mixture of a mother's pride (at least what she assumes a mother must feel) and of the wonder one feels when they are experiencing something new—a slow climb to understanding. It is that feeling of when the world in front of you feels both so big and so small at the same time (two dimensions fighting each other inside the frame of your sight [are your pupils dilating?]).

Down here, a person could get tired of floppy-haired boys with faux-English accents and their long-lean girlfriends. *Dude, you're from fucking Detroit.*

Art is artifact. Art is art in fact. Starkness, expression, a shock, distorted bodies. Earlier, she and Delores were watching an old BBC documentary on Francis Bacon. Chimera fell in love with him immediately. He reminded her of her grandpa or any grandpa in the sense that he was so appreciative to speak about his thoughts and theories, and how he was a real person with his slight self-deprecation and asserted truths on what *is* and what *isn't*.

"I am a person who has had a lot of luck and a lot of chances." Mr. Bacon said, propped up at the bar of an English pub.

"Why is chance more important than conscious intellect?" asked the reporter.

"Because... I have made images that intellect would never make."

His goal was to create "not illustration[s] of reality but to create images which [we]re concentration of reality and a shorthand of sensation." How lovely.

This memory would be the last time that night that Delores even remotely crossed her mind. The singer came down from the stage and three girls were up there now, pressing buttons in the dark. The singer was her friend Finnegan. She was swaying there, leaning near him, and trying to remain a part of everyone else. The whole damn'd crowd—

She was drunk now. It didn't take long. He took her hand and led her away.

Oh, quaint little Ludlow (bricks and bricks). My ethnic Clinton Street (always some drunk yelling, the cars entering Manhattan, the colors, and Spanish teenagers) where Mapplethorpe took his nudie pics and Cohen dreamed of ladies. Finnegan was walking her some place—more than likely home. Looking up at his pale face, its soft brown freckles and square black frames, Chimera felt the compulsion to capture it like a butterfly in a glass jar.

And we're made to think of art as being something superfluous.

What happens when you realize you are a burden?

Oh, well. [Time to [Fuck] it all].

4.

"DAMN IT! HOW WILL I EVER GET OUT OF THIS LABYRINTH?" – SIMON BOLIVAR

Here kitty, kitty, kitty.

A young Arthur Noyes was laying on his stomach in a pile of hay on a humid July morning in the barn on his father's property in Eustis, Maine. Imitating the soldiers he had seen in the World War II movies, he pulled himself through the starch, yellow trench on his belly with his elbows. He extended one chubby, freckled arm coaxingly towards the tiger-striped kitten that toyed a few feet away.

Much earlier on, Arthur had been sitting in his father's living room watching television. It was a special occasion because Father rarely allowed such treats. That night, however, he had come into Arthur's bedroom very, very late to wake his son. Together, they sat silently in the living room, alone, watching in amazement as men with great bubble heads padded weightlessly across the screen. Arthur's Mother was sick at that point and she had stayed in bed. She missed the whole thing.

"Do you see that Arthur?"

Seated on the floor, Arthur turned from the screen to look up at the great, scraggly mountain of a man. "Yes, Father?"

Father cleared his throat. "A man can do anything he sets his mind to. There are no excuses." He then leaned further back in his old stuffed chair, closing his heavy lids. He lifted a gigantic palm to rest on the protrusion of his bare stomach. He burped.

"What do you want, Father?" The words shaky, tested the waters of unprecedented conviviality between Father and Son.

His Father's eyes opened slowly. "What?"

"What do you want..." Arthur repeated. "In life?"

Stilted awkwardly against the moment, Father slowly replied, "I just want you to be a good boy."

The pat of his gigantic hand on the knee of his jeans summoned the boy. There was an unfamiliarity that made little Arthur's movements jerky, each step frightened but excited. He couldn't help but smile at the surprise recognition he was getting from Father. He pulled himself up onto the hard angles of Father's lap. Father's jeans smelled like the insides of empty, old beer cans, a tinny, molding must. Father closed his eyes again and, keeping them shut, asked Arthur what he wanted.

Arthur paused and really thought. Then he smiled. Clapping, he squealed, "I want to sing and dance like Gene Kelly!"

The eyes reopened, glowing though yellowed. Veins chaotically swam towards his black pupils. They turned down to look at his small son as Father encased Arthur's shoulders between two massive fists. As the shaking began, Arthur felt a severing inside that only two hands can produce when put on another person. Father abruptly stood up, his hands round Arthur's thin neck, moving him back into the chair. Standing in front of him, the hands moved to unbuckle his long, leather belt.

After Father had gone to bed, the son spent the rest of the morning outside crying until the Sun had fully risen and he lost interest in his tears (one of childhood's greatest blessings). He climbed the ladder to the loft, deciding he was going to play with the newborn kittens. Arthur finally convinced one to pay enough attention to him and scooped it up in his tiny hands. The kitten he had gotten his hands on was suffering from a common barn-cat disease called panleukopenia. It made the animal very weak and, consequently, easier to grab. Its eyes were almost completely crusted over, bulging out of its sockets like tiny rotting grapes, and it struggled to breathe through the phlegm built up in its nostrils. Arthur either did not understand or chose not to acknowledge the fact that his new friend was sick and he laughed when the snot bubbled out of the struggling animal's nose.

"Mr. Bubbles". Arthur declared to no one in particular. He played around with it, with Mr. Bubbles and his suffering, for a few moments by dangling a solitary piece of hay just above the lethargic but haphazardly frantic daggers that searched the air. He laughed until he was bored again and then Arthur decided it was time for a new game. In the barn, he was the big one and Arthur Noyes decided that it was time to get serious.

Frowning at the kitten, he suddenly threw it to the ground. The force with which this helpless thing landed stunned Mr. Bubbles and the floorboards cradled his confusion. Before it could scramble away, Arthur picked it up once more and placed its frail body in one hand and put its objecting head in the other. As he pulled, a tear ran down his chubby, red face.

"You fucking queer."

Perpetual.

* * *

Arthur Noyes was now the sweaty old man who watched over a mother's shoulder as the next person in line, a freckle-faced nine-year-old, shifted his weight in boredom, pressing his slender thighs from side to side. Unknowingly, all eighty-seven pounds performed a stilted dance in the sunlight and Arthur couldn't help but smile at the lack of grace. *Whoever humbles himself as this little child is the greatest in the kingdom of Heaven.* Blessed be He whose innocence exudes His Beauty!

A lot of children have unpleasant childhood memories. For instance, Pesach Numen, and his sister Mary, had been adopted by their uncle because their mother was incapable of happiness. It is a common human disease. Three years ago, Arthur's considerably younger half-sister Margaret had, all at once, lost everything of value in her life; her marriage, her temperance, her job, her beauty, her sanity, and, eventually, her children. When Arthur went to pick up the children that December, they found Maggie sprawled unconscious on the ground. She hid camouflaged on the wood floor, wearing only a khaki raincoat and the same baby vomit and cigarette ashes that were spread throughout the barren apartment. The girl, then a toddler, was sitting beside the dead, drunken moans of her mother. Spit bubbled complacently out the side of her mouth as she looked up at her new father and giggled.

The only people Arthur could truly even

stomach being around were children. He knew that others judged him; that some even thought he was crazy. Yet, the children danced about, in streets or stores or pews unnoticing, free from those worries. They listened to what he had to say like he had authority. They were pure innocent beings, like Arthur had been once for a very short time. They frolicked about like asexual nymphs, ignorant of the world's toils and thus happily and perfectly innocent. The world was still their Eden. Inside, hidden away, they had a locus amoneus. All they needed was love and Arthur, as the corporeal embodiment of the greatest love of all, was going to make sure he loved every single one of them. They needed his love.

His heart raced as he saw the bus pull up to the sidewalk and the children began to mill in for afternoon Bible study. Pesach and his sister jumped out smiling, and Arthur could smell their fresh skin from the other end of the walkway.

"Here kiddies, kiddies, kiddies."

5.

EMILY DICKINSON SAID, "I MUST GO IN, THE FOG IS RISING."

"Do you believe in kindred spirits? Something in him was familial to me."

Chimera remembered the morning she met Arthur vividly. It was the beginning of the worst week of her life.

* * *

Acoustic guitar.

It's nice to lie next to another body.

The blood drained in her hands and feeling returned to the tips of Chimera's long, white fingers again. Two yellow bodies curled up into each other. A moment of quiet chaos, silent. Words would have littered the air with vulgarities. Silence held such potential and, besides the sighs and wet moans, left each movement up to interpretation. *This ethereal haze....*

She pressed her naked body against his as she slipped her arm underneath. Warmth. She touched her lips lingeringly against Finnegan's bare back in arbitrary places. She felt him, knowing he didn't love her (she waited but it never came), but she also knew she would not replace this moment in her life to be with anyone else. Exhaling, Chimera closed her eyes.

He is asleep now.

***

It was what her skin looked like underneath—a pale green-yellow surrounded by the inflamed white perforation of her broken skin. It was like peeling back the layers. This was what she looked like under the excess of pale flakes that formed her being—a moldy yellow, creased and cracked, etched with blood, rotting from the very onset of generation. She had no idea how she got the cut on her knuckle. She just woke up one morning, heavy and foggy-headed with a hangover, and found it consuming the whole midsection of her right middle finger. She could have burned herself while drunkenly attempting to light a cigarette. Maybe she unconsciously blistered it from sliding her hand continually up and down some stranger's genitals. Maybe she contracted a flesh-eating virus.

Outside is an eternity of dust, thought Chimera.

Things like this kept happening since Delores had stopped speaking to Chimera. Sometimes she unconsciously ripped out her hair, piece of piece, strand by strand, and she wouldn't even realize it until there would be a small bald patch. Luckily, as of yet, these patches have always appeared under the crown of her head so she was forced to wear her hair down constantly in order to cover the spots. She wouldn't feel pain, she would be completely enraptured by whatever she was doing—reading, writing, some solitary action because it never happened in front of anyone. It was an itch, a deep itch. Suddenly, there would be a break in her thoughts and she'd look down and see a bundle of tenuous black hairs stretched out across the gap between her breast and shoulder. She would hurriedly pick them off, filled with disgust, and then rubbed the new bald spot contemplating what had just happened.

Moments of stress. She was constantly destroying—unconsciously ripping off tape, destroying restaurant napkins, drawing on library desks, digging her fingernails into anything malleable enough to acquiesce to their strength, tearing labels off beer bottles, chewing the ends of her pens, picking her cuticles to shit, carving obscenities into barroom bathrooms like a degenerate.

"It's a sign of sexual frustration," Finnegan told her.

"Thanks Freud."

But now even he had stopped talking to her. No one was around. It was her and this room. She thought of Gabriel often, picturing raccoons in a garbage dump. She thought about how all of them rotated around each other, bumping off each other—Finnegan, Dolores, silence, this city, herself and the baby Gabriel she placed in a trash bin. She thought about how death comes in many forms.

That night at Pravda, when Chimera went home with Finnegan, was a Saturday. Delores and Chimera had a long-standing date that Sunday morning, every Sunday morning, without fail, they went to the same Brooklyn church that Delores grew up attending from the hours of 8-9:30am.

Chimera woke up curled on the floor of Finnegan's apartment in Bushwick at 8:45am with a horrible headache. If it were not for the panic and hurry, she would have recognized the full-body cringe that had nested itself inside.

Thankfully she was already in Brooklyn. Sprinting down the broken, uneven sidewalk, Chimera made it to Our Lady of the Rosary by 9am. She slipped into the last pew looking like the wet garbage that gets caught in a storm drain. Chimera tried to wipe under her eyes and finger-brush her hair down inconspicuously. Glancing over, she noticed a man staring at her from the distance of half a pew. Besides herself, he was the only person seated in the back of the building.

Chimera avoided eye contact. She turned her head to search for the familiar sight of the back of Delores' head. There was a horrible taste in her mouth. She settled into the familiar feeling of being so far away from Delores.

They had all been friends at one time—Delores, Chimera, and Finnegan. In fact, Delores liked him better than Chimera had at first. Chimera was annoyed that he called them Dolly and Mrs. Miyagi. "Wipe on, wipe off." He'd laugh. It changed—the dynamic of their triangle—one weekend, a year ago, for no real reason. Unless alcohol counts. They were seated in the night, the summer heat reverberating off the pavement to incubate within their clothes, holding sweaty glasses and smiling against the soft light from the street and candles on the table. Surrounded by others, their problems evaporated with their sweat and the laughs rang soft and light in the dark amid the clanking of glasses and flatware, the murmured conversations, and the diligent black. A lull flew in with the insect, its wings spread brown and grey, winding through the air capriciously like the conversation it had stalled. The crowd's attention followed the arbitrary movement of the moth as it circled the group, flitting slowly across the table.

Delores smiled, her warm brown skin glowing in its beauty while the others faces remained stolid but contemplative, eyes dancing with the small, unexpected addition to their gathering. The solitary candle that burned in the middle of their table sat naked as the flames removed its layers, white wax poured over the edge of its base and spread across the table until it became solidified. It looked like roots, thick fingers grasping to the table. The moth came closer and closer to the candle until its thin, pounding wings beat against the light.

From where Chimera was sitting, the moth's body was in front of her and, when the wings separated and spread open, she could see the colors disappear, leaving only thin, veined curtains glowing white, painted in light. She closed her eyes tightly as the moth suddenly plunged its delicate brown body into the fire and all she had for confirmation were the gasps of those seated around her. In the fire, it sat without struggling as the burning ate her, the wings gone violently with only a moment and a wisp of smoke. Chimera opened her eyes as the remnants of the body tumbled from the wick into the liquid running towards the roots. As it got further away, the wax slowly moved over its corpse, blanketing it in white. By the time it reached the base, it was completely immersed in the solid roots and everyone finally looked up at each other.

"Jesus." Chimera said like it stood as an all-encompassing thought.

"Yeah," Finnegan laughed. "Weird."

Chimera laughed too, leaning her long neck back and shining the whites of her teeth. Her hand fell and rested on his. The alcohol was dulling everyone's actions and her body moved to stretch out before his eyes, much like a suicidal bug. *Good luck.* Delores looked down at her drink, tried to ignore the obvious actions of those who surrounded her, and realized that, at that moment, she never felt further from G-d. Not so much because she cared about Chimera anymore or about Finnegan but more so because she didn't care about any of them at all.

Abruptly, the staring man moved closer to Chimera and this realization moved her from her thoughts. The Father's voice rang from the pulpit, incandescent and even, like an omnipresent buzz. From the corner of her eye, she saw his pale skin punctuated with beads of sweat, his round shoulders and glasses and thinning blonde hair that was more like an illusion of hair, baby-white-blonde, like gossamer. She turned to face him straight on and noticed that his eyes pointed out on two separate paths, making his head seem more curved and giving him the unfortunate stigma of all lazy-eyed, patch-wearing, false-eyed people—that being one in which people have a hard time trusting someone who cannot look them directly in [both] eye[s].

Leaning over, he whispered—"You don't believe this bullshit, do you?"

Chimera opened her mouth but could not think of anything to say. Much like Arthur would continue to do throughout the rest of their relationship, his blunt, enigmatic statements left her genuinely speechless.

6.

"HERE IS A PRESENT FOR YOU."
- GOEBBELS

Genesis 8:8-12 says *"And he set forth a dove from him, to see if the waters were abated."* For the past three hours, Arthur had been traveling to his sister Margaret's house. It would be almost exactly six years from now when he would meet Chimera Aoki. When he picked up his new children, they would be a family of three. His new daughter was

three and six months. He was surrounded by threes, though he did not know it yet. He would see it eventually.

Come on, come onnn.

Arthur Noyes was standing in the narrow cubicle, hovering above the toilet and pulling on himself, leaning all his weight on one arm; the middle finger and thumb of his left hand formed a tight circle. He squeezed his eyes shut and grit his teeth into a strained smile. His movements were manic and his thoughts bumped haphazardly from image to image, trying to latch onto something substantive. But he always circled back to the comb, moving back and forth like waves in the sea, pushed by a thin, white hand—sometimes he saw the little boy, his face punctuated by siren cries.

There were three stalls in this men's room. Arthur had chosen the middle one because he never went into the first (the most used) and the other was a handicapped stall. It was nicer inside the tighter space anyway, felt like less air existed in there, a little bit like choking. The metal had been painted green, sloppy with streaks and age, and the white tiled walls were etched with thick brown grit. Sweat beads formed between the blonde strands of Arthur's thinning hair as he feverishly tugged on what felt like bread dough. Despite his best efforts, there was the faint noise of a man holding his breath (the breathing in, the sound of the lack of sound) coupled with something close to a wet napkin being flattened (repeatedly and rhythmically—*squish, squish, squish*). After a few moments more, struggling in vain, Arthur paused, leaned his head down a bit and let a large glob of spit fall into his open palm.

When Arthur was a child, every night after dinner his mother would brush back his hair with one of her silver decorative combs. In the summer, they'd sit on the porch, he on the lower step, both of them facing the same direction with Arthur cradled between her knees. Mother would take the comb from her pinned-back hair and drag it slowly across Arthur's scalp as they talked of the day or as she sang or as they sat in silence watching the sun set.

The comb was about four inches wide with a dove etched into the handle, nested between scrolls of Art Nouveau thistles and fleurs. His mother wore it almost every day, the grey face of the dove peeking out from her hair. When she died, it was the one thing Arthur kept. It sat in his desk drawer now. But he still saw it when he closed his eyes—the dove's black eye and pointed face. In between the imagined genitals and moaning, it kept surfacing—the dove flying at the behest of her long fingers. Arthur grew frustrated. If he stuck his stomach out as far as he could, he couldn't see his erection. He opened his eyes for a moment, looking down, and there was nothing there but movement off the horizon. When he closed his eyes again, Arthur could see his mother's hands rubbing that protrusion and then moving slowly up his chest to his throat. The frustration began to subside.

The door inside the gas station bathroom swung open with a proclamation of hinges and quick-moving feet. The other man's breath was heavy and even. He moved into and latched the first stall. Though nothing in the second stall paused, the thought of how many germs lived in the first stall flashed across Arthur's mind. He heard the weight of a large man falling on the seat, the stranger's weary sigh.

"Fuck," the voice muttered lowly on the other side.

Arthur squeezed his eyes shut and, holding his breath, moved faster. Something was happening now. In the darkness inside him, images oscillated between Mother and genitals and the idea of his son. Sometimes a bird flew in. Sometimes images of a large man on the toilet. Jeans around thick ankles. Maybe a moustache. Time was at once rattling and lugubrious in the black. People, real and fake, alive and dead, came in and out whenever they pleased.

There was straining on both sides of the green wall that separated them. The stranger tried to escape it but Arthur tried to lose himself in it. He had a son now. A son of sorts. A little boy had come into his life and Arthur would seize the opportunity to shape him into something greater than himself. He would cry for hours when Arthur cut all the evil away, like it was an irreparable loss. A death of sorts. Arthur would move along that boy's body with the same thin white hands as his mother. The same white hands pulling and pulling now on something stronger than it had been before. A parent is an adult who shapes the life of a child. Grooming, one might call it. There was a prolonged grunt from next door and the splash of release. Arthur's whole body contracted. Surrounded by shit, a white dove flew forth—finally released from the long, white fingers.

A death of sorts.

It smelled like rot and salt—just like the sea.

7.

AN UNFINISHED NOTE BY HART PEASE DANKS –
IT IS HARD TO DIE ALONE AND

"Sometimes, I have this reoccurring dream where I'm in this large wooden room, like an abandoned barn with these old grey boards curling inward, the rusty nails freeing themselves from stability, hanging red precarious spikes, and in the middle of this room is the gigantic spool of yarn—it takes up most of the room and floats off the ground because a large metal rod attached to either side of the walls pierces it, holding it closer to the ceiling. So I'm in there and it is just the smell of mildew emanating from the cracks in the wood, the yarn and two men—I know one is my friend Finnegan but I can't make out the other. Suddenly, both men stand up, looking at something I can't see and they're mesmerized, they're moving closer towards it and I try to follow but the spool of yarn starts unwinding and I get covered with giant waves of purple and orange, black, blue, and greens.

The harder I struggle to see what they're looking at, the more yarn enfolds me but I'm kicking and gasping in this awful sea of color, trying because I know whatever they're looking at is beautiful.

So it goes on like that for a while and, though there are no windows, I can tell the days are slipping past, but I don't give up, I have to see. I've got the will, you know? The worst part is I can't swim, so I dogpaddle until finally my legs cramp up and my head goes under, lungs filling up on the monotony of each day struggling to find beauty but, day after day, to be only surrounded by the color bruises."

* * *

Chimera felt the need to get out of there. She woke up very early. 5:15am reminded her of some strange cadence. An opus ending as she watched the sunrise with tired eyes. It broke in uneven geometric shapes above the buildings in the distance.

She had once read the New York was for "the free; the poor and the young". But Manhattan can be a very claustrophobic place—it has the unique ability to feel both infinite and insular at the same time. Chimera supposed it is the way a lot of people feel about their lives and where they live but there is something about this city that made her feel like it was the whole world, like all of civilization was stacked on top of itself and teetering on one small island and the rest of the Earth was a wasteland, desolate like the surface of the moon. There were a lot of lines there, strong hard delineations, black and greys. Outside, the warm haze and the sea. There was an inexpressible pressure from above.

To someone else across the world, this place is exotic. To someone travelled, places begin to all seem the same.

Delores was raised to go to church so Delores went to church on Sundays—that was all there was to it. It was something she did because it was a part of her. It was less than twenty-four hours later but they were already heading back for Christmas Eve mass. Delores had barely spoken to her in the past day and in their tiny apartment, the season seemed very dismal. Though her emotions no longer stretched to extremes, it was obvious that Delores was more than frustrated with Chimera's tardiness to church the previous morning. To make it worse, Chimera still felt sick and was not sure if she had gotten over her hangover from Pravda or if it was something else.

It was dark and wet on the corner of Clinton and Houston ("How"-ston) and they both had to step over a small embankment of snow to get into the taxi. On the way to service, only directions punctuated the silence until the driver clicked on his radio and *Fairytale of New York* came across the speakers.

"I love Shane MacGowan's voice," Chimera said after a moment of listening. "It's not beautiful or particularly melodic, but there is something within it that is so melancholy and romantic." There was a pause. "He sounds like a real man."

"What the fuck is a *real* man?" Delores spat towards the window, her face turned away out towards the river and the black lines of the Bridge. Chimera didn't know how to respond—she had gotten used to talking to herself. She shut her mouth with a soft popping sound and turned towards her own rain-speckled window. When the song broke into a crescendo, it briefly made her picture Finnegan's soft, stupid face—always smiling. The goddamn Irish—their bittersweet lives. Chimera only let the thought of him exist for a moment before asking about the strange man that she had met that Sunday.

"That's Arthur." Delores said, again without moving, but this time without venom. Delores knew Arthur from her support group. Another long-standing appointment Delores had was to attend her support group every Tuesday evening from 7-9pm in the basement of the church; though this was a tradition where Chimera was not invited. Delores went there to speak about the scars on her face. Upon second thought, Chimera decided not to ask what was wrong with him.

"He volunteers with the youth group." Delores added.

"Oh. But what does he *do*?"

"I don't really know."

The image of Arthur kept creeping back into Chimera's thoughts, replacing other faces, including her own. He was an unattractive man and seemingly common, someone who looked like any other average middle-aged white guy. But there was a fervor inside him that Chimera found appealing. He seemed very real. For a few minutes before the end of the service, Arthur had talked about the importance of creation; that making beautiful things made the world better. Chimera told him she was an artist—a writer—and his eyes widened. Delores had never cared about art; from their first date in front of Bacon's tritpych, she made it clear she didn't understand the fuss. She was more concerned with cleaning up messes, bringing things back to normal. After years together, Chimera grew to realize that what Delores had done to her face was more a matter of righting a wrong than creating something more beautiful, as Chimera had first thought.

Arthur seemed more passionate in that brief meeting than Delores had been in the whole three years that they had been together. He wanted to make something new, Chimera wanted to live to inspire a thousand songs, and Delores wanted to put each note back in order. *One of these things is not like the other.* She couldn't remember verbatim those fleeting moments but the essence of his sentiments lodged itself deep inside the pit of her stomach.

When Chimera first moved to New York, she made an effort to meet artists, to go to galleries and warehouse parties in Brooklyn. None of artists she met went to art school. Most weren't really artists. Some were rich and just wandering; others were poor and just wandering. They were very nomadic, her 'artist' friends. They moved in and out of her life easily as well. They all loved altars and black and cigarette smoke. They wore rings and charms that beat against their chest as they pounded throughout the city. They had holes in their clothes and they legitimately didn't give a shit. She didn't know how most of them lived in this city (the poor ones at least). No one had a 9-to-5, everyone was at home smoking weed and watching movies or researching the possibility of alien life while she sat behind a computer in her assigned spot among a span of cubicles stretched out in the grey monotony of corporate forever. (The worst part about the cubicles was that she was surrounded all day by people who thought these meaningless exercises were important; these people enjoyed Starbucks and malls. They were people who listened to and legitimately enjoyed the music played on the radio.) At her grey desk, she would daydream about getting a tattoo on her neck of a Munch fetus Jesus.

Life being a brief light amongst the darkness of eternity, and I choose to be here, edging closer to getting my candle snuffed out, shuffling papers and sitting through meetings where I have to breathe in deep and remind myself to be polite to these cunts.

She came to the conclusion that this innate compulsion towards responsibility was a horrible affliction. So instead of sitting there at work and cursing her friends' disregard for convention, the jealousy seeping, she quit. She wanted to focus on her art. But art is amorphous. It is unpredictable and, because of this, she never formed a plan. This last fact infuriated her parents. When the news reached them, they never responded. And they never would again. The elder Aokis abandoned her without a word. It was disturbingly easy. Like they had just been waiting for disappointment. Chimera lived now like a bored housewife but younger and more lost in terms of defining any meaning. It wasn't long before Chimera realized she had never known such complete sadness. As much as she hated to admit it, she was lost without convention. It was impossible for Delores not to be resentful, since she worked as a nurse and spent long hours wiping up shit and puke and all the other putrid liquids a body contains. And each night when she got home, Delores found Chimera had grown into an even sadder and more despondent person. It was infuriating until she decided not to care anymore.

From the second story of a small apartment building, Chimera's view of the Lower East Side was either the snow-laden borders or a handful of white blossomed trees like umbrellas over the parade of bass-pumping cars and sweaty, passing hipsters, or older Latinas, their flesh rising between elastic garment cinchers. Strutting like peacocks, these New Yorkers—everywhere the eyes and, thus, the desperate, ever-present need to have something to look at; be it some extra flesh exposed or bright pink hair, some reduced to screaming into their cell phones like anyone gave a shit about the minutia of their lives. Auditory ejaculations, visual foreplay—*we see you, we see you, we get it. You're great—how unique.* Chimera found it harder to be original—she fell back into the words of others for comfort. This book she was writing was supposed to act as an impetus to something more—her own words made permanent, so that they existed outside of time. Inspiration.

However, Chimera got stuck there—in the lives of other people, much in the same way as Delores was constantly cleaning up after others. Except Chimera didn't fix anything; she just documented it in essentially a large list as she looked out her window. Delores' window. But all biographies end the same way, don't they? And it was difficult to constantly see death looming over these lives. It was frightening. No one seemed to understand it either. Since Delores had no connection to art, nothing to say one way or another beside to ask Chimera to put her books neatly in a single pile instead of strewn across the apartment like leaves in autumn, Chimera thought she could show it to Finnegan, since he was an artist, and get his thoughts. That's how she prefaced the first time they had slept together, a few weeks before the night at Pravda.

"Ah, yes. Let us return to your

pagoda." Finnegan pressed his palms together and bowed as they got up to leave the restaurant.

How can you be racist and live in Manhattan? Chimera looked at his glowing dappled face as he hummed *House of the Rising Sun*. Anti-Semitic? It's like being a misogynist who chooses to live on Lesbos.

She felt as American as anyone. She grew up in the suburbs for Christ's sake. So it annoyed her when Finnegan pointed out her difference. There was something about him that made her sick {it had always been there} but she still took him home to the apartment (Delores' apartment) and slept with him. It was almost same type of satisfaction she would have had had she slapped him in his face.

Delores was still at work and, afterwards, when Finnegan had left, Chimera would lie in their bed and feel disturbed about her lack of remorse. There was a complete absence of guilt; though she knew Delores did not deserve this, it didn't feel wrong, but it didn't feel right either. It was Nothing incarnate. Because there wasn't anything to break. Or so she thought.

As soon as they are inside, Finnegan's first question was "What's with all the books?" He gestured to the loveseat, stacked with biographies.

"I've been trying to work on a book of last words."

"What do you mean last words?"

"I mean the final words someone says on their deathbed, right when they're about to die."

"Aren't most of 'em 'oh shit'?" He said 'oh, shit' punctuated.

"Some of them are really beautiful and profound. Hobbes is said to have said, '...A great leap in the dark'."

"Hm." It was curt and she couldn't tell if he was thinking or just placating her. He was looking down at his phone.

"Eugene O'Neill said, 'Dammit—born in a hotel room, died in a hotel room.'"

"Who is Eugene O'Neill?" Still looking at his phone.

"Dude—really?"

He shrugged in response. He was tapping on the phone's screen. So she turned back, and said lowly, "Shut up."

He finally looked up, tucking his phone into his back pocket. "Sooo... what's the point of this? That even great men feel pathetic? Death is universal?"

"I guess it's more about your last thought, ... the last chance to stamp some meaning into the world."

"Before you fall out of meaning."

"Exactly."

"If no one is there to hear it, do words even have any meaning?"

"Mmm, touché my little cumberbund."

"Mon petite cannonbear."

"Mais oui," she sighed.

Chimera often worried about the possibility of spending her whole life (however long it lasted) on a piece of art and never finishing. She worried about it at that moment too when Finnegan's lack of interest became apparent. Once she started compiling this list of words, she realized that it could go on forever. The manuscript became a living thing that fed off the dead. It grew limbs and pulled itself in all directions. She contemplated the title being "Polymelia."

"Onward Christian Solider." Delores said flatly. The words brought Chimera back. They had arrived at the Lady of Our Rosary.

A strange and awkward ache silenced Chimera as Delores paid and moved to get out of the cab. The church felt like a lonely cantata with a shy vibrato, the recapitulation of "shining, shining" like a fading echo.

I AM A NOUN. So is this place. A mass sequestered from the heavens. Simple people, simple pleasures. Everything was everything and always will be.

The church sat in a silent part of Brooklyn, hidden like a pensive child, peeking out from behind stunted factory buildings and warehouses. Its jutted, imperfect stone wall caught small fragments of streetlight and the albedo made the churchyard glow a light blue. The sidewalk outside the sanctuary was severely neglected, soft brown orbs and veins of the earth below seeped through the cracks and holes in the pavement. Outside the entrance, Delores rested her hand on the short iron-gate surrounding the blue trees that shivered in the wind, and she looked across the snow-laden yard, towards the pariah. It did not seem to be disturbed by being an anomaly except for the want of upkeep it was lacking. It just sat there in a contented grandeur that evaded all of the other square, uniform buildings that mimicked each other until this part of the city was covered by millions of ugly, unfeeling brown and grey replicas.

Delores admired her sanctuary from a distance, softly smiling as she turned to see Arthur's shadow fall against the glass. She moved towards the entrance. The children were moving in behind, the stunted exodus from minivans and subway tunnels moving towards the light emanating from the opened doors. Arthur stood laughing, talking whole-heartedly downward to his young flock.

Delores turned to Chimera and, for the first time in three days, talked to her without malice. "Do you want to formally meet Arthur?"

She didn't wait for a response. They moved right behind him in line. He stood there with a girl and a young boy. The thought that they did not look like they belonged together crossed Chimera's mind.

"Arthur," Delores called, loudly enough to get

his attention. He stood three steps above them as he swirled around, frowning. "This is my girlfriend—Chimera Aoki. Chimera, Arthur Noyes."

Chimera instinctively stuck out her hand and Arthur smiled. "Oh yes. Hello."

Their hands touched briefly.

"And who are we?" Delores asked. She bent her knees to create a face-to-face level with the children.

"Introduce yourself." Arthur said, looking down at the girl.

"I'm Mary." She was a ways apart from her brother and Arthur. The brother stood nearly on top of Arthur.

They exchanged pleasantries. The two grown women turned to the boy and waited for him to introduce himself but Arthur interjected first.

"This is Pesach," He said, grabbing the boy's shoulders. Pesach's eyes drifted to the ground. "He doesn't speak quite yet."

Delores and Chimera nodded, forced smiles politely. They all continued inside and took their seats, with the Noyes family a pew in front of the girlfriends. Chimera looked at Pesach and Mary and thought about the trinity in front of her. Pesach looked to be about five or six years old and, while Chimera admittedly knew very little about children, she was surprised that he was unable to speak based on his size. Was he simple? Or deaf? Or disabled?

At the end, there were cookies and tea in the Parish Hall (aka the basement). It was past midnight but children still milled around in laughter. Arthur moved towards her against the current of bodies. Delores had left her almost instantaneously to speak with a group of women.

"So you said you're a writer?" Arthur asked.

She reaffirmed that she was, smiling at the interest.

"I am too," He said smiling. "It is hard to be a creator, to be responsible for lives outside your own. Real or imagined, there is a dependence on you. Which can be good—it makes you powerful. But it is difficult nonetheless, having lives dictated by your words. You must live up to it. Your word."

Arthur then started a diatribe: about the sermon, about effective writing and what he thinks is the purpose of art. Chimera was a willing audience. She smiled genuinely for the first time in months. It was a surprise critique, like school but in practice.

"Listen," He retorted at one point to someone who was not there, the S full of spit. "Don't talk to me about G-d. Just don't. Don't fucking do it."

Chimera laughed but she wasn't sure why. She felt similarly, though again she was unsure why. *Why the hell are we here then?*

"Did you know we know the exact date of the

Crucifixion? [Chimera shook her head] It's April 3, 33. Do you know how they found that date? [Chimera shook her head again] You use the moon and the historical dates of Passover."

He had a gravel voice, not like Johnny Cash, something more sinister. He had a heart-broke Tom Waits voice. She smiled at his animosity and they continued a one-on-one conversation in their own corner. Tête-à-tête. She spoke very simply, like an adult would to a child, and it was oddly placating—the even beat of her monotone. Their two voices, though an octave apart, seemed to achieve a synchronization. Their words entwined.

At one point, Arthur asked, "What's your favorite parable?"

8.

"TEXAS... TEXAS... MARGARET."
– SAM HOUSTON

Arthur's Mother died in February of 1970 and Father had remarried by October. Arthur's new mother was seventeen years old at the time; she was almost eleven years to the day older than Arthur. Her name was Annabelle Leigh. The only trait she seemed to share with Father was that she moved past Arthur silently like he was a shadow. Arthur went from being part of a triangle to being a lonely star orbiting two distant planets. He thought about his first Mother often; the memories did not seem to slow down. In fact, they kept building up like some nightmare. Most people in mourning know that it will come to an end, that "time will ease the pain", new things come along and hopefully you can forget. But that never happened for Arthur. The memories kept circling and, as they flashed, it was impossible to tell between what had really happened and what he was creating in his mind.

One day, just as Arthur approached puberty, Annabelle announced she was pregnant.

"You know what that means Arthur?" She and Arthur were alone in the kitchen.

Frightened by the attention, Arthur turned to look towards the floor. Annabelle reached out suddenly and grabbed his face, pinching his cheeks with her thumb and forefinger. "Look." She said, jerking his face towards hers. She released him and removed a glass from the cupboard, filling it with water from the sink. Annabelle slammed the glass of water on the counter and Arthur watched the water rock back and forth.

"A woman is born like a glass of water; she is pure and clean." Annabelle said, looking down at him as she reached for the chives growing in a small pot on the sill. She tipped its murky water and bits of dirt into the calming water and Arthur watched as the soil particles swirled and dispersed into the clear body. "And this is what a man is. Something that ruins us until we're something no one would want."

She left the glass full of dirty water on the counter and walked angrily out of the kitchen. He listened to her muttering dissipate down the hallway (something about thirst and the need to get clean).

***

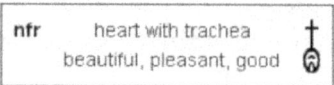

nfr	heart with trachea
	beautiful, pleasant, good

Arthur had always believed in the power of symbols. The magic of an icon. Since he was young, he always seen more in images than other people. Subtle movements. Double-entendre. Other people seemed to pass by without seeing what was around them, the hidden meanings that existed everywhere and in everything.

When he moved from the farm to Brooklyn, it took him a while to find the right place to live—one where he wasn't constantly barraged by blinking lights, bodies milling, and ads pasted on ads. T-shirts and electric signs and cigarettes. Slogans everywhere—all very explicit. There was nothing to read, no interpretation. It was all for the gut (or the dick) and nothing for the brain.

He settled in Greenpoint with the Poles. He made a good choice because Manhattan only continued to get louder and more compact but 116 Oak Street aged without much change. No one spoke to him in a language he understood and it moved slow enough for him to truly see everything. He was only a block away from the water.

It was a good place to raise children. Pesach and the girl had been with him for more than five years now. Their mother had had them living in an apartment below train tracks in Camden, New Jersey. The other half of the duplex had been boarded up when he got there. As far as Arthur was concerned, it could not get more depressing than that.

Here they were left alone while still remaining a part. A stone's throw from the best city in the world. Or worst, depending. When Arthur thinks of the impending apocalypse, it gives him great comfort to know he could watch it swallow Manhattan from the shores of West Street. It would be a transmogrified landscape where the outline seems more distant but would provide an uninterrupted view from a row of broken-down factories. There would be no more fences, no more condominiums—just grey skies (fire & foreboding) and the abyss of forever, rocked gently by the soft waves of the East River.

Arthur arrived in the city and wanted to get things in order. He wanted to make something truly great. To take all the Fathers and roll them into one and really bring the world some peace and light. And every journey begins with one footstep. The first step, his first real opportunity, lay within his home. The tattered brown, two story building in the middle of Oak Street. Manhattan was once a wooded island, isolated from the rest of the world (before it became the world). Rome was founded based on the whims of a riverbed and a den of wolves. Bethlehem, a few huts and an empty barn.

You need to be able to hear the messages. G-d speaks to you randomly in short inaudible missives. A blind prophet is worth as much to the world as an unassuming one. Arthur's entire body flinches in full fulmination when they come through. A man's body, internally, is a cross—with the crown on the head, two appendages reaching outward, towards the other lines, and it ends at circle. It implants itself in a symbol that means forever and everything. Or the vast nothingness. In a woman, that circle lands in one of three places: the throat, the heart, or the womb. In a man, that circle lands one of three places: the mind, the heart, or the scrotum (a circle that holds two circles that holds more circles within circles themselves—this is where all life originates). The heart is obviously the best place; it is the closest humans get to the Holy Spirit. All other destinations root the body in confusion or illusion.

The first time Arthur had seen this message written down was at his Mother's funeral. The symbol was sewn into a purple blanket that lay over her coffin. She looked like she was sleeping underneath it. The face of (presumably) the Virgin lived inside the circle. The emblem could look like a crucifix at the top of the world. To the Egyptians, it meant an absolute Nothing. Upside down, it was *crux ansata*, the symbol of Venus (a fist clenched shut, a gaping hole).

If you move the cross inside, it becomes a warning. But Arthur saw what it really was immediately; he just innately *knew* what it meant.

It was a map.

It took Arthur a long time to decide what was the best plan. He spent years searching for more messages. And they were everywhere. He would ride the subway and take buses to their last stop before they circled back. He gathered them in a notebook, filled it with faces and words and images and definitions. But he had to read them carefully to make sure he was doing it correctly. He had to *really* think about everything [every thing]. Eventually, he found that the best messages find you.

All the time he knew that to make something better, you had to try and take away what was bad. Clean it up, make it prettier. Create something truly pure. The girl was now almost nine and Pesach was five. It took them about three months before they would refer to him, without prompting, as Father. It was good to get to them while they were still so young. Children are highly adaptable. Malleable. Eventually, he had gathered and analyzed and finally determined what was right. What was best for all of tHEm.

Like a rotten tooth in the mouth of humanity, you had to extract the rot to preserve the rest. Arthur knew he would have to weed out sin from whence it originated. Circles encircling a circle and so on. It was a violence but with love; a holy kiss (en philemati hagio). But it was not a love with violence (en philemati agapes).

He realized what he had to do on Christmas Eve 2012 (21 12 2012 2012 21 12 12 21 2012 || 22 12 2012 2012 23 12 12 24 2012). He saw the final sign in Chimera. It hung between her small breasts like a mirror.

9.

AGRIPPINA, TO HER ASSASSINS. *"SMITE MY WOMB."*

Chimera woke up late in the morning on Christmas Day. Delores was already gone—to where Chimera couldn't say. She had no one else to talk to that day, since her parents had stopped returning her calls a few months ago. So, out loud, to herself, she said, "Merry Christmas." Chimera pushed herself out of bed. She folded the screen of the room divider back and moved to the kitchenette/library/living room/office area for breakfast. A small box of strawberries sat waiting on top of the microwave. Chimera smiled. Once in a while, there still were small tokens of affection. Delores was a wonderful, thoughtful person in many ways.

She had supported Chimera to the best of her ability and especially when no one else had. She made a Sisyphusian effort to roll Chimera back to life. But no one, no mortal person, could tolerate that torture forever.

The strawberries were like death rattles that gave Chimera small moments of hope that their relationship might be able to be mended. Before she moved towards the strawberries, Chimera went to the bathroom. She pulled out a cardboard box from a plastic bag and shook it. Then she carefully removed a test from inside a foil wrapper, like a present. After, she sat on their love seat with Delores' Shih Tzu Samson, and, as she pushed one red body after another into her mouth, she thought about what might be next. By the time Delores came back home, Chimera had finished the entire box. Delores had a bag of groceries and, nodding hello, she began to unload it, spreading the food out on the floor in front of the refrigerator.

"Have I told you my theory?" Chimera ventured an offering. She was trying to decide what to share with Delores.

Delores was slow to respond. She had begun peeling a carrot into the sink with long, slow movements. "What?" She asked, obviously bored.

"You completely replace every cell in your body every seven years. Every single cell is a different cell. It's this constant decay of our bodies. It enables growth." This thought elicited nothing from her audience. "So now, you take someone like you, 35 years old."

"Yes?"

"So.. you have been five different people during your life. You have been five entirely different people."

"I don't know." Delores replied, filling the space. She wasn't impressed.

"Yeah—think about it. You shouldn't have to be accountable for acts committed seven years ago. This whole thing proves the uselessness of marriage, monogamy, um... our jail system. And sin."

"Don't you think we carry on the same ways of thinking... or emotions... what about memory?"

"Are you anything like the person you were seven years ago? Or even a year ago? There is no stability!" Her voice reached a disingenuous emphatic peal.

From the dark of Delores' back, Chimera heard her say, lowly, "You just don't want to have any responsibility for anything."

Chimera started to cry, hard vibrating sobs. Delores looked up shocked but didn't move towards her. There was a great stillness outside Chimera's vibration.

Chimera choked out the words—"I'm pregnant."

"Immaculate conception?" Delores was always quick. Chimera could never read her. Was she mad? Delores may have been trembling imperceptibly.

"I'm sorry."

"You're an idiot." Delores turned suddenly and began moving things around in the kitchen. She pulled something black from the drawer. "It's over. You know that, right? It's over. This is it. You have always been a child."

That was it. Nothing angrier—no shouting. Chimera was a child. With a child. A line spiraling into itself.

An ouroboros.

Within fifteen minutes, Delores had gathered all Chimera's books into garbage bags and placed the bags in between them, her arm extended out in front of her, pointing. "Goodbye."

"I don't know where to go." Chimera felt like folding into herself and her words came out slow. "I don't have any money." To Delores, it sounded like a child whining.

"Well, I guess it's about time you get a real job and figure it out. Like the rest of us."

When Chimera walked out the door, with three black garbage bags full of books and papers and clothes, Delores called out to the back of her head with that slight twinge a voice gets when it fights back tears.

"Merry fucking Christmas."

The door slammed closed and Chimera stood in the dirty hallway for a moment, not knowing what to do, because this was the first time in three years she was the one facing away from Delores.

* * *

For some reason, Chimera felt like a doctor's office should be some holy place—immaculate and white. But they are always rooms like any other room. Chimera noticed every mark on the wallpaper and floor. Old tape on the cabinet that no long held anything but itself to the wood.

I didn't kill you; it's more like I threw you away. (a dent in the doorjamb) *And, in some ways, that's worse. Because it might seem like there was a complete lack of emotion—perhaps it was feigned for the sake of my sanity or for some manifestation of greed—but, in the end, it was comparable to tossing away a used razor. Buried in the bottom of a trashcan, next to the used tissues and nail clippings is a baby—a life that I created and removed from myself to place in another adulterated womb.* (a slow drip from the sink) *Encased in a uterus of discarded napkins, needles, and apple cores—my baby is there waiting for his chance at life, for his chance to fuck it all up. It didn't feel like a baby. You were just a lump of cells.* [You are just a lump of cells]. *Like a sneeze into a tissue—part of my lungs/brains came out.*   *Awh*-**choo**. *Awhf*-**Wiedersehen**. (a discarded rubber glove hanging over the edge of the trash can—two of its fingers pointing at her).

It is very easy to stay in a relationship—there is a comfort even if some part of you knows it is toxic. You could wait an entire lifetime and let everything just happen around you. A routine can placate the most tormented soul(s). *Rock-a-bye baby*.

When Chimera closed her eyes, she wrapped her arms around her stomach and hugged herself. Against the pain, she whispered, "*Gabriel*."

* * *

Finnegan opened his door but never gave her a key. There was, however, a half-hearted "Welcome my little China doll." It was 12.27.2012 (indivisible) and in the space of three days, Chimera had lost family, friends, places, and the time that filled in between the events. When she returned home from the doctor's office, Finnegan was out with his roommates. Her three garbage bags were stacked in the corner of his apartment at the head of the couch, where she had been sleeping rather than in with Finnegan.

They had had a conversation the moment she reached his apartment on Christmas Day, looking for any port in this storm. He made it clear that she could stay for a few days but it wasn't a permanent solution.

"Why?" She had asked. "Why am I not good enough?"

"Because," Finnegan said, looking straight into her eyes. "I feel like the world owes me." He shrugged his shoulders and that was that. An arpeggiated chord.

She closed her eyes and a pointellistic wave of green-blue hues swept over, undulating softly against the black like moss at the bottom of the riverbed. It was the ensuing strange and painfully awkward sinking feeling that silenced her. She felt the sick happiness found in the empty, hollowed-out emotion of profound loneliness. What got her here was undeniably her fault. But partly it wasn't. She felt lost. No one had ever told her that she would have to carve out new paths. She thought life was serendipity. Like Art.

And so far her life seemed to have been surrounded by infantilized men, stunted by a hypersexuality (*the access to pornography maybe?*). They seemed to be grown men but sat in the laps of fifty-foot women. Nothing real was satisfactory anymore unless their whore became their mother or some sort of more grandiose monster.

Chimera had given up one creation for another. He laughed at the pages clamped together with a large, yellow binder clip. And we are made to think of art as being something superfluous.

What happens when you realize you are a burden?

Somewhere across the East River, at the same time, Delores was having this conversation with a friend.

"Part of me thinks she got pregnant for attention."

"You are giving her an awful lot of credit for having any forethought."

Chimera sat on his old couch in Bushwick and felt worlds away from everything she had ever known. Something inside her felt like it had died. Is it possible that your body can start to decay before you are fully dead? That part of you dies before the rest? Yes. Inside her womb was rotting away. Black as cancer.

She sat there, hunched over, alone, with Finnegan's laptop open, looking for jobs online and pulling out small patches of her hair. Strands gathering into a black pool. Patches expanding like white pools above her ears. Yin-yang. Everything and nothing. You and me. (a) Holy fuck.

It was at that moment, all alone, quiet and fading—that her phone rang for the first time in months. When Chimera looked down at the phone's face, a series of numbers popped up and above them, in bold black lettering, it said **UNKNOWN.**

10.

שָׁלוֹם

שָׁלוֹם

שָׁלוֹם

WRITTEN BY ALBERT PIKE

Arthur and his children lived on a street where all the houses are white. At least, some shade of white. Except for theirs, of course. Their house was brown.

A house has so many lines—horizontal and vertical lines, intersecting lines, loose, scraggly lines of wires and rope. A face not so many. Or at least we're tricked into thinking there's not so many, far away, just a smooth openness punctured two-times-twice underneath an uneven blonde hairline. Like the inside of a seashell—there's a gloss, a faded pink.

Esse est percipi.

Arthur often meditated, to himself and to his children, in that brown house, on the idea of being and not being oneself. The divided self. Interior/Exterior. Understanding the intangible side of you; born broken from a wh[0]le. It was in this brown house that he finalized his Master Plan, though it was years in the making.

Ever since he was young, Arthur had to fight against the darkness of his thoughts. Stroking a cat's leg and thinking it felt like a leg of chicken. Like eating meat. The disturbing calm that overtook him when he thought about slicing his wrists (always three lines, both arms, thin perpendicular lines—a tattoo) and pictured himself bleeding out on a bathroom floor {in his mind it felt like a deep exhalation}. The thought of knowing you have the power within yourself to kill someone else—that murder wasn't something that existed outside the self. To really hurt someone else. And how easy it would be. The act. Arthur was constantly frightening himself—the thoughts visiting him arbitrarily, whenever they felt like it. Sometimes, if he squeezed his eyes shut or hummed against their noise, he could shut them out.

But only sometimes.

He learned in Group (en masse) that we take our

rage out on those closest to us and we take out our love the same way. He met Delores Maranatha there—in the basement community room at Our Lady, in a group for people trying to understand themselves. Most of the people there had done something horrible to themselves while trying to figure out who they are. Delores had filled her face with scars; Arthur, his wrists. Rending flesh. In his mind, Arthur justified most of them as acts of flagellation.

Arthur had once told the Group that he feeds the malignancy within him until his teeth could not longer gnaw through the black. Everyone sat around in silence, as eyes rolled and brows arched and gazes fell to the floor. Delores was the one who finally spoke.

Who says that? She asked.

No judgment, Delores. The director placidly reprimanded her before moving on.

Last Saturday night, Arthur had had an abnormal dream. All of Group was at Mass but no one else was there. Except Our Lady of the Rosary was not the stone and stained glass and the ratty maroon carpeting and plastic flowers—it was a whitewashed, bare Puritan sanctuary with crystal acicular icicles hanging from the rafters like sharp diamonds. The only thing that remained the same were the pews; old and mutated and worn from years and years of use. The gnarled wood wrapped around Arthur and pushed him further into his arid seat. The parishioners, scarred and sacred, became skittish with seizure-like movements. The congregation—now epileptic—began to cling to the walls with some invisible magnetism. Their frantic bodies slowly rose towards the ceiling, shaking like live crawdads. Mouths were gaping open and shut like land-born fish. *Where's the preacher* Arthur called out. The shakes, a trembling delirium. He closed in his eyes and when they opened again, he was in the backseat of an old car next to his first Mother, a range of mountains in the background and the flat, sad infinity of middle America spread outside beyond them. It was calm and silent except for the sound of tires moving against the pavement. The panorama spread out before them without interruption because no one was in the front of the vehicle. *Where's the driver* Arthur called out again with the same terror and the same immobility. His Mother turned to smile at him, her hair brushed back with a silver comb, but when she moved her mouth, all was silent except the noise of movement—the wheels on the road.

Halom halamti. What does it mean? What was his interior self trying to tell his other self? What was he trying to say to himself?

The next day, no one from Group was at Church except for Delores, who almost always sat up front. Arthur slid into one of the back pews as usual, several pews away from the rest of the audience. Pesach and the girl were safe downstairs in Sunday school with the other children. Arthur wouldn't want them to hear what was happening up there anyway. It was usually an atrocity of interpretation. Translated into and from a vulgate. It takes an artist to understand the multiple layers of meaning within a word.

Arthur was at a liminal stage of his life—an age where he should be married, emulated, or immolated. He had made a plan that involved himself, his son and Father. It was the beginning of making the world better. It was relatively simple but he still had to bring himself to do it. To create this ideal, this beauty—like an artist. Something real—no trite fable. It was all there for Arthur. Yet something felt like it was missing. Was it the driver? The preacher? A speaker directing the masses?

A young woman slammed her body onto the other end of his pew. She was wet from the rain and her swollen eyes were red, perhaps from crying. She was strange, someone he had never seen before but much like other New Yorkers—wearing all black and pretending not to notice him from the corner of her eye. It may have been her youth but there was something there that drew Arthur closer. It shone from the bright foliage of her face. She too wasn't listening and she looked rather suspicious in this setting. In fact, he couldn't tell if he was drawn to her through longing or suspicion, though he supposed the two go hand-in-hand.

He moved closer to her to ask what she was thinking. "You don't believe this bullshit, do you?"

She finally turned to show the entirety of her bright face. Her eyebrows arched as her mouth opened but no noise came out. Finally, she made a noise like a disgusted laugh got stuck in her throat. "No, I don't."

"Then why are you here?"

"The same reason as you are, I suppose."

"I doubt it." He smiled in some way that could seem either coy or evil. They spoke in murmurs for the rest of the sermon, buffered by their distance from the others. They spoke of art mainly. At one point, he recited a poem (it was *No Coward Soul is Mine*) by heart.

Clearly impressed, Chimera smiled with her whole mouth. That was it. That was all he needed. A glint of light from her chest caused him to glance down, where he saw a small, silver circle with a cross growing from it. It was the final sign.

He saw her again, only a few hours later, on Christmas Eve. She stood with Delores but Arthur could feel the distance between them. It wasn't subtle. He also saw the way this young woman looked at Pesach, intensely and almost with awe, like she had seen something holy. They spoke more that night, secluded again from the crowd, and he learned her name. Chimera. Chimera Aoki.

He saw the potential in her that passed by in other, more mechanical girls. One could see the emotion right on her face. It was in her attentiveness, her ability to actually listen to him. It was the way she looked at him. The attention that s/he needed. She could make them move out of the stiff structure of a triangle (three straight lines) into a circle. Or maybe a lemniscate. At any rate, something more fluid. A mirror into and outside of themselves.

Chimera had given him a series of numbers (10 in a specific sequence). Arthur chose to dial them when he couldn't find her at service the following Sunday. Delores was there, unsmiling, in the front row but no sign of the lithe black cloud that had covered the back pews the past few times. Third time was not the charm. When he called her that Monday, he wasn't sure what he was going to say and when she answered, all he could hear were her tears.

"Why weren't you at Our Lady yesterday?"

She cried softly for a moment before she responded. "I don't believe in that shit, remember?"

Chimera went on to tell Arthur about her troubles, most of them anyway. How Delores had thrown her out, how she had nowhere to live and no money. Like an abandoned child. An abandoned 28-year-old child. (Four different 7 year olds). *At what point are you no longer an orphan?* Arthur wondered. He considered himself one and had for a long time, ever since his first Mother had died so many years ago. Though it had taken her a while to speak, through her tears, once Chimera started, it didn't seem to stop for quite a while. She seemed drunk. Arthur sat silently on the other end of the phone, in reality only a few blocks away from her, thinking about how this was another blatant sign. The phone call, the numbers, and the mirror. Our Lady of the Rosary. He had to save her. She was meant to come into his life. He helps her and she helps him. He needed help but more than anything else he needed an audience. That is the basis for all relationships, isn't it?

She showed up at his house later that night with three garbage bags. She had walked to Oak Street and she was covered in a light mist of sweat. The children stood behind Arthur in great interest of this creature, alien to them in almost every way. It was dark outside but Chimera seemed to be radiating. She and Arthur spoke in few words. Chimera basically thanked him repeatedly; different combinations of words but all with the same basic meaning.

She was indeed drunk but, to the children, who had not seen a drunk person since they left Margaret back in New Jersey, she seemed silly with sleepiness. With her three soft boulders of possessions placed on the couch behind her,

Chimera jerked her face around and focusing on the children, knelt down suddenly on her knees and hugged the girl tightly. The young girl looked concerned and did not move, keeping her arms loose at her sides. Chimera released her thin frame and turned to face Pesach straight on—the placid, numb-faced changeling with his grey eyes and caul-covered mouth. "It's okay." She whispered, reaching out softly and wiping his small lips with two fingers. "You're a good boy, Gabriel." She kissed him directly on the lips and pulled back slowly, smiling with her whole mouth.

She stood up again and looked up at Arthur. *Is it her soft, sad joy that reminds me of my Mother?* She obviously saw something special in Pesach as well. In him, there was a part of Arthur. In him, Chimera must have seen a part of herself. *Why shouldn't our youth(s) span generations?*

Arthur moved her bags and gently led her ignorant but willing body towards the small room below the stairwell. It was white and empty except for a naked bulb, a pile of his books and papers, and a blow-up mattress with thin beige sheets that had the faded outline of seashells flanking its edges. An over-turned plastic tub sat like chair in the corner. This room was meant to be his study.

Arthur moved outside the door, again in between her and the children. She stood framed in the dark, looking around with a face that seemed like all thought and feeling it once contained had now evaporated.

"Are you going to be alright?" Arthur finally asked.

She smiled at him again. "I yam what I yam." Shutting the door, she left Arthur and the children out in the soft yellow light of the living room.

The girl appeared at Arthur's side, and tugged on his shirtsleeve. "Father, do you want to see what I learned today?"

Arthur pulled his arm away but nodded. *M-hmm.* She moved to stand square in front of him like she was prepping for a performance and he looked down at her like a spotlight. The girl pushed her index fingers into the corners of her eyes and said in a slight sing-songy voice—

"Chinese {pushed up}, Japanese {pushed down}, look at these dirty knees."

Arthur didn't respond further than a nod. He walked by her but couldn't help the thought. *What does that even mean?* Was it/it was a{n obvious} reference to Ms. Aoki?/.

All that girl has are two white legs and a restless soul. He had insisted that Chimera move in to complete their circle. It felt like the right thing to do. It made him close to happy. She felt the same way. Four makes a circle, not a square. Or maybe a triangle to hold the fourth above them with the strongest support possible. Chimera Aoki was the last missing piece Arthur Noyes needed to carry out this long-incubating plan.

It is important to remember that we take our rage out on those closest to us. And we take out our love the same way.

11.

"BELOVED, THAT WHICH CAUSES LIFE, CAUSES ALSO DECAY AND DEATH. NEVER FORGET THIS; LET YOUR MINDS BE FILLED WITH THIS TRUTH. I CALLED YOU TO MAKE IT KNOWN TO YOU." GAUTAMA BUDDHA SAID.

Before she went to sleep, in her haze, Chimera opened up her bags and took out all the loose papers. Everything she owned was intermingled in that muddled, black womb. Chimera luckily had the forethought to number the pages of her manuscript and, now, she took her time to carefully arrange the pages in the correct order. She made a second pile that was for loose notes and images or photocopies of text that she used for inspiration. It took about an hour and a half to get everything in order. She then stacked her books in the empty corner based on size and placed all of her clothes in one bag. Last, she placed her manuscript pile and notes pile in front of her wall of biographies.

Looking down at them, she felt the physical manifestation of this journey in the number of pages that grew from the floor. It was a monument to her exploration. It was early the next morning before she actually lay down on the air mattress to sleep. Sitting up, she pulled the drawstring to click the light off. She was almost sober by then.

Still, as she lay down, her thoughts turned only to Delores no matter what distractions she tried. Chimera opened her eyes to the black and reached out to feel the absence of Delores in front of her. Curling inward, she tucked the seashell sheet into herself. It was so quiet in Greenpoint. The room vibrated with absence.

Chimera thought of the time before she knew Delores, when Delores was a stranger and she was simply passing her free time by trying to figure out what she wanted. She supposed she was still doing the same thing but this was before she had really experienced loss. One Fall afternoon, Chimera sat on the bench outside the dog park in Tompkins Square Park. She read this exact passage before she looked up to see the mass of black curls framing Delores' unique brown and pink striped face.

"but as I pass O Manhattan,
your frequent and swift flash
of eyes offering me love,
Offering response to my own—
these repay me,
Lovers, continued lovers, only repay me"

Chimera looked up, her finger holding her place in the book, and scanned the park to rest her eyes. They landed on Delores, standing over Samson, smiling close-mouthed and distracted. She looked dark-skinned and serious, and her face was punctured by thick ribbons of keloid scars that worked themselves indiscriminately across its plain. Chimera was at once mesmerized by that face—how different it was, how it wore its fallibility so unflinchingly loud.

She found herself in New York at an inopportune time and in the most clichéd position for a young person who believes they are an artist—she was destitute, relatively lazy and thus uninspired, living in Brooklyn with a series of boyfriends. She was a bit narcissistic but without any self-confidence, she was somewhat ambitious but with little follow-through, and she was hungry to be something unique in a city where everyone else is trying to do the same thing. It was a lose-lose situation and overall, her own problems were starting to feel exceptionally mundane.

Chimera had spent more than twenty years being intimidated by men (friends, family and lovers). She was just beginning to see that they were actually all just little boys—peacocking, but desperate for some attention. She acted as the perennial mother figure, and yet she still felt the compulsion to strike a balance with also being their little girl. Ma Donna, Ma Meretrice (Ma Mere Triste). A pat on the head, her fingers running through their hair. Shh, shhh.. *It's okay, it's okay, it is all going to be okay...*

Every man is a child, a skin never shed. A woman, however—she breaks away from the seed, blooms—bold and unknown (a brief moment in the sun), and then folds into an extended decay.

When Chimera first met Delores, it was very different. Delores did not look at her the way a man would. In her hands, Chimera felt an actual comfort. There was a solace. Delores took Chimera the Museum of Modern Art for their first date. It was there, under Bacon's triptych, that Chimera learned that Delores had scarred her own sacred face.

*   *   *

"New York has become, for me, a series of boxes. Boxes upon boxes, transported in boxes to more boxes—lines and concrete and metal that lead to more lines and concrete and metal. And

I'm not complaining, I'm just seeing more clearly the lines every day. It's a grid and, had I a more mathematical mind, I think it'd be processed easier. I just see it through the ways I was taught, as an art student in college, to see the line ("Really *see* the line, Chimera"), the objects in front of me as a series of lines within a series of lines—the depth, the space or the lack thereof.

Having to constantly strike a balance between 'live for the day (today)' and 'plan for the future'—and those who don't believe in 'back-up plans' usually don't believe in luck—but are surrounded by it. Luck is a gigantic component in success, I don't care who says otherwise. I know because I've met quite a few unlucky people, whose talent and wit never aligned with Time and Space. Who were poor or ugly and, sometimes, even worse, both. Who simply never had the 'right eyes' <u>see</u> their work or potential. I've also met people who have 'had success'—who were also lazy or unmotivated or talentless. These people were often attractive but the one thing they all shared was that they were all lucky. They were born into certain families, or had met certain people—they had been born with a certain amount of symmetry in their lives that most people never attain. Complementary lines.

I remember the first time I met Delores Maranatha.

Was it luck? It felt like truth."

* * *

Sighing heavily, Chimera was close enough to see the tiny crystals of salt still sitting complacently on Delores' fingers. They were sitting in MoMA's café and Delores was eating French fries from a paper plate. The right side of her lip had been cut halfway to her ear and now Chimera lifted her eyes up, thinking it looked like a healed smile, one that had stretched too far, one that had forgotten its boundaries. She held back the compulsion to reach her fingers up to lightly touch the flesh worms working their way across her skin and read Delores' face like Braille.

Delores finally looked up, and noticed her new friend staring at her. She smiled sadly, and thought that Chimera looked so sweet, so young and desperate. Yellow jasmine was tied to her wrist by a thin, white rope fraying and curling in the flowers, up the stem. She was talking steadily about Francis Bacon's Three Studies for Figure at the Base of a Crucifixion. How it represented space and performance and corporeal sacrifice.

"It gives me that weird feeling of when you're traveling and when you have that realization that—I'm in *this* space right **now**. I occupy this space in the world right now. It's mine." Chimera stopped looking at her, turning her face away. She was quiet for a moment. "Don't be mad."

Delores thought she smelled oranges, the citrus spray of its broken skin. "What?"

"Can I ask you about your scars?" A purity.

Delores took her by her lightly fragrant hand, small and white and delicate. They left the museum and made their first trip together outside of Manhattan. Delores took her to meet a man at Mount Zion.

* * *

"You want the story of Delores? That girl who broke her face? It's tragic. She ruined a true gift from God—that beautiful face. But she couldn't destroy those green eyes of hers—they still show like the soft, sparkling moss that grows at the bottom of a brook. The kind that hide in the crevasses of cold, dead rocks but cannot stop from gleaming like strands of emeralds when the sun breaks through the sky." He paused for a moment with a slight, sad smile worn on his face. They were at the nursing home portion of Mount Zion hospital. Delores worked there as a nurse. She was now taking care of the people that had taken care of her as a child. A concentric citadel up on a hill (working downward).

The old man shook abruptly, turned his focus back to Chimera, and said bluntly, "She took a steak knife to her face. They say she tried to kill herself, but I don't think so. There were no marks anywhere on her wrists, her neck. She called the ambulance herself. "

"So, what happened?"

"No one really knows. She won't say for sure. It

was just a normal night. She called up the cops and we came, Frank and me. We were the first to arrive and we found her sprawled on the dining room floor. She was wearing a cute little housedress—it was white with a pink bow at the waist. It was covered in blood by the time we got there. It was a shame. It was a cute little dress."

"Was she conscious?"

"Oh, yeah. But in shock, I think. When we came in, we had a hard time finding her at first. We were running around trying to hear her screaming or crying, But Frank found her by following the blood. She was by the kitchen sitting on the floor with her legs spread out before her and her elbows dug into her hips in order to prop her hands in front of her face. But she wasn't crying, or screaming, she just sat there very calm with her blood-stained hands folded in front of her face."

"What was she doing?"

He looked away from a moment and furrowed his brow. "Well, I don't really know but it sure looked like she was praying."

Chimera paused, reflecting. "Praying?"

"Well, her lips weren't moving and she was completely silent. I don't know for sure. It was just eerie. We burst in there in a hurry and when we found her, she just sat there very calm with her eyes dead ahead. We all stood silent for a moment—Frank and I were so taken back by her demeanor. The whole situation was so stupid really; it was almost comical. Frank and I stood there, two big guys, frozen solid, looking down at this small, delicate body with a face like an open gunshot wound. She looked like a doll, thin and white and fragile— with that cute little dress on. But her face—"

He swallowed hard.

"God, I've never seen anything so awful in my entire life."

Far past the grey living room of the ACE Unit, his eyes searched somewhere unseen. Eventually, they met Chimera's and she could feel the hesitation. He cleared his throat in anticipation of tears.

"She ripped these huge gouges into her cheeks and forehead and took a good chunk of flesh out of her nose. And the blood just ran everywhere, down her neck and her sweet, little dress soaked up the red. Her hair was starched with blood—it stood in jumbled clumps solid. As I said, Frank and I just stood there dumbfounded before she slowly blinked those large green eyes and looked up at us. Those eyes awoke something in us; they lit the room on fire. We snapped back to reality. Frank looked through the kit for something to clean up her face. I started to move her to get her into the ambulance and when I leaned down to pick her up, I said something before I realized the words were coming out of my mouth."

"What'd you say?"

Mr. Conejero squeezed his eyes shut and shook his head. "I said something to the extent of—'Why, why would you do this? You're almost unrecognizable. I walked through the door looking for an angel but found a monster instead.' And I swear to all things holy, she turned the congealed crimson jelly of her face towards me and smiled."

***

"There you have it." Delores said as they left. "Straight from the horse's mouth. I don't really remember. (she shook her head) I wasn't really there."

***

Chimera Aoki suffered from a rather common problem.

She could make herself fall in love with anyone. Men who treated her badly, women, old, and young. It took very little to maintain/retain her affections.

((PAY ATTENTION TO ME))

It took even less to convince herself of love. A sick creature that could subsist on feelings of repulsion and worry and that most treasured sick feeling of loneliness and worthlessness and sorrow—in the same way that you grow to love the feeling of being hungry, if you persist through it for days and days, or running or anything else that tires the body, strains it to exhaustion.

She hadn't gone there knowing what would

happen—the will just found her; new in the alien sense, isolated and strong. Some moments proceed without its participants being fully cognizant of themselves. More than lost in thought, a kind of temporary insanity maybe, but more real– like the tangible tremble of rage, a sudden burst (passion as a violence concentrated). Insanity implies having lost something, these fits are of something misplaced. In all truth, that was exactly it—she had gone there expecting something, the expectation allowing for her to misplace that awful feeling of love. Delores didn't have that *je ne sais quoi*—she had a brazen *je m'en fous*. It felt infinitely more real than anything else she had felt before. Her face was a map to a mirrored internal torture. Chimera selfishly thought it was so romantic.

I will always believe that there is beauty in the incomplete.

How did that rapture fade into Finnegan saying "Let's go Tokyo Jane." and her actually following those vile directions?

All of these moments had brought her to this squeaking air mattress on the floor of some stranger's apartment.

Was there a purpose?

Was this meant to be?

Had everything happened for a reason?

Did she act as a pawn in larger scheme? Or was

she a protagonist that carved her own path? Made her own meaning?

Now she knew she should have said no. Could have. No. Something more guttural—Uh huh her, Hey Hey My My, verbalization of vowels, the heavy dirges discordant mixture of sharps and flats—*I don't think you understand, the love I feel is stronger, I feel more, I feel it all*—the last living girl in New York, her face was a mosaic of scars, rough night, silent night, kick drum, a sprite, punch-drunk Irish lovers, ad infinitum...

As she looked back, she said,

Follow me.

Although she already knew Delores was gone.

She was asleep now, both further away and still so close.

12.

IN AGONY, "A LADDER, QUICK, A LADDER!" - GOGOL

A barn owl got trapped in the house the day Father died. Barn owls are white birds with blonde bodies. Their faces are shapeless, pure white masks with two black slits for eyes. The sharp V of its beak hides underneath a sheath of white feathers. When it opens its sharp mouth, it sounds like the cries of a wild Irish banshee: mournful, tremulous shrieking.

Annabelle thought it must have gotten in through a hole in the attic. She made it very clear that it was Arthur's job to remove it, while she and young Margaret hid outside, picking blackberries. Father was still upstairs; his body was laid on his made bed, on his back, with his hands folded across his stomach. He was wearing jean overalls over a collared shirt. Though his eyes were shut, Father still had the countenance of an impatient man waiting.

Arthur walked through the rooms upstairs, armed with an old broom that he carried like a flag. After he had paused at the open door to his parent's bedroom, one thought kept repeating itself as he moved around, slowly so as to make the least amount of noise on the wood floorboards. That thought was—*I don't have a Father. I don't have a Father. I no longer have Father.*

Arthur had woken up at dawn that morning with a strange feeling. Father hadn't been sick and there was no outcry when he had been discovered. There were no tangible clues that something monumental had happened. Instead, a pale sun stretched across the dusty brown sky and cast a light across the land. A thick, residual heat remained from August's bitter end. It radiated off the earth from in between the brown blades of dead grass and stalks that stood, barren and splintered.

In a brown room, on the table, sat a bowl of fruit and flies.

And Arthur could smell death.

What do you do when someone dies?

Arthur didn't know. Annabelle wasn't sure either. She washed and dressed the body while Arthur waited downstairs with the baby. As she finished, Arthur heard her scream and come tearing down the stairs.

"Goddammit. God-*damn*-it." She said angrily when she reached them in the kitchen. "There's a goddamned owl in the house."

She picked up Margaret, wrenching her from Arthur's arms. "Scared the shit out of me." Annabelle instructed Arthur to catch the animal and release it outside. She grabbed a large, metal mixing bowl from the cupboard and left with Margaret's chubby, toddler legs wrapped around her hip, one arm implanted firmly on the backside of her diaper. There was no discussion. Arthur did as he was told.

As he walked around the house, Arthur tried to remember what the last thing Father had said to him. The last piece of meaning he had stamped into this world. What were the last words they had shared between them? What had they shared between them? He couldn't remember right away. All he could think of was—*I don't have a Father, I don't have Father.*

What was the last thing they had been talking about?

The day before, Arthur spent the day with Father, working on the hogs. They were about four months old now. First, Father and Arthur separated the ones that would become barrows from the rest of the herd and guided them in the barn, sequestered away from the rest in the back.

Father usually grabbed the closest animal and pushed it down, on its back, holding it there for Arthur. Most times, the pigs just lay there without struggling. They either didn't know what is about to happen or they didn't care. Maybe it was so inconceivable that fear did not even cross their minds. Arthur would kneel down and feel their underside for the testicles.

"Make sure you get both of 'em." Father had said.

Arthur counted each time. One, two. The testicles squished in his fingers. There's one. There's two. He held them both in his hand. He opened a metal clamp that stretched a small rubber band so that Arthur could place it around the pig's soft flesh.

Do you know what a Burdizzo is? It is a device made of metal. On one side, there is a handle used to apply pressure, like brakes on a bike handlebar. On the other, there is a clamp the opens in the middle in a small circle. Whatever you put in the circle can be squeezed as much as you'd like. Farmers use it to 'modify their crops'. Father didn't like doing it that way. He preferred the bands. They suffocate that part of the body until it died and fell away from the rest of the living. It takes away what you need most. Blood. Air. Proximity to a beating heart.

The whole ordeal used to make Arthur very sad. The   idea   of   changing   these   animals permanently. Maybe it was more the lack of cognition. But each year, it kept happening and nothing changed. Perhaps he became desensitized to it. Perhaps he saw the blessing each change bestowed. How in ignorance they never had to fear the change. How they could be made better with one knowledgeable movement.

Sometimes, when Arthur was walking the fields, he'd stumble across a necrotized piece of flesh, tied off at the end with a green or yellow rubber band, like a dead balloon. Most times, though, he never saw them again. They faded away from meaning soundlessly.

Father had done the same. Quietly, in his sleep. Part of him had died years before. Pieces of him kept flaking off into infinity. The most tangible example sat pickled in an old jar atop the kitchen hutch.

When Arthur was very young, Father had an accident with a piece of farm equipment. It sliced three fingers off of his left hand (index/pointer, middle, and ring)—all three clean off, the first two right at the knuckle. When Arthur thought of Father as an adult, he would picture the stump of the ring finger slamming into the tabletop when emphasis was needed. Or used as a blunted instrument to point at whatever item Father focused on at that moment.

Father had gone out to the barn that morning singing "The Wild Rover".

Arthur's first Mother hated the idea of losing part of Father. In the chaos of blood and bellowing cries, his Mother had scooped up the three appendages and slipped them into a jar, along with some vinegar, salt and cloves. Over the years, the skin puffed and flaked away, until it collected white and yellow sediment at the bottom like an ugly snow globe. But Arthur's first Mother refused to throw it away and, once she died, Arthur's second mother kept up the tradition, moving the jar out of the way though, but still allowing it to peaceably continue its slow decay.

Arthur was still upstairs when he heard the inhuman cry from the kitchen. He moved quickly downstairs and scanned the room from the doorway.

"Hello?" Arthur asked the room. There was no answer. The kitchen sat as it always had ("always" being relative solely to Arthur's experience). There was no discernable movement until Arthur glanced up to Father's fingers sitting in the pickle jar. The kitchen hutch almost reached the top of the ceiling; it left the space of about a foot. Up there, directly atop the old pickle jar, sat the stolid, arched body of the white barn owl. For a moment, it looked like Lot's wife, solid as a statue with an intense marbled glare of longing and suspicion. Arthur lowered the broom and stood cowering under its gaze. The bird had the important parts of Father's left hand under three angry, curled talons of his right foot; holding each other (reciprocal) or holding the other (unrequited, unequal).

What the hell does that mean?

Arthur moved very slowly towards the window that sat above the sink, the whole time keeping his eyes on the owl. When he reached the window, he didn't take his eyes off the black slits that followed him across the floor from its perch above. Arthur blindly reached for the tongue and pulled up the glass and then pushed the screen open. Fresh air rushed inside; it smelled faintly sweet and earthy. As he moved his hand back to meet the broom, Arthur accidently bumped the handle out of his other hand and the broom hit the floor with a large rap (RAP, rap-rap, silence).

That was enough to startle the white statue; it let out one of its ugly cries as it spread its wings out to expose its full span. As it moved, it kicked out the jar from underneath his foot, and it fell the entire height of the room and shattered on the floor. Arthur, who wasn't really thinking at this point, in this space of seconds where his thoughts did not have time to form, didn't move much, though he did hunch further down, bending his knees and bringing his arms towards his chest, so that his hands were holding each other over his heart. He looked down at the floor to see Father's fingers glossy as fresh fish, tossed on the floor in the middle of a wreath of light and sharp-angled shards.

The moment immediately after it broke was completely silent, save Arthur's labored breathing. The white mask of the owl's face stretched with his body and its eyes bulged in a stunning blackness. As Arthur breathed out, it swooped down in one graceful movement and picked up two of the three fingers and arching up, seamlessly exited in one excellent rush of air out the window. Arthur's breath came in again as he looked back down to the puddle of juice, glass and skin flakes in the center of the floor. The last sad piece of Father lay there, a nub of the ring finger pointing out past Arthur, facing towards the open window.

"Gee whiz." Arthur said to himself and the empty room. He grabbed a dishtowel that lay over the faucet and using it as a barrier, gently picked up the last finger and, without rhyme or reason, tossed it out the window and shut the screen again.

When she came back in, Annabelle made sure to clean all surfaces in the kitchen with bleach. "Those things are riddled with disease." She said.

She swept away the dirty puddle without question. It smelled distinctly like rotten eggs. The remains of the jar were tilted into the trashcan and they tinkled away into infinity.

A trio of men came later that day to pick up Father. They drove away into the sunset, the dust billowing out behind them in polite, swelling curtseys. Bright waves of gossamer.

Father's funeral was very simple. A wooden box and no ceremony. The awkward, angry triangle of Annabelle, Margaret and Arthur (misshapen— Pesach and the girl hiding inside). A stone rectangle topped with a lunette was imprinted with a cross and stamped with Father's name and his dates (numbers arranged to have meaning). The odd sensation (table's turned) of looking down at Father as he sunk in little shudders into the earth. Father had always loomed over him like an inescapable mountain range. But now there was only a prairie, vast and boundless. In it Arthur was as tall as a tree, spreading his roots ever outward, only hindered where the earth became lost to the sea.

The pastor did speak. He said a few words though they were nothing about Father. They were about G-d and His Mercy. He referred to Death as a reward. The pastor tried to buffer the sadness with some hope in an unknown happiness but, at that point, Arthur the young man felt the furthest he ever had from G-d or any notion of a god. A shallow madness quelled inside, washing against the soft shores of his experience. He thought about why he felt such hatred towards this old man. Was it his ignorance or more his presumptuousness that bothered Arthur? Was it that Father lay dead and they were told to be happy? Grateful even?

Looking past this scene, this odd ritual, down the hill towards the harvested wheat fields with the sun shining and birds singing, Arthur knew he had just lost his faith, in any recognizable form, whatever little had been instilled in him throughout his childhood. Arthur no longer needed to listen to other men tell him about salvation. He would find his own way there. So he turned his thoughts to his Mother and imagined the sea.

Hail Mary, full of grace, the Lord is with thee;
blessed art thou amongst women,
and blessed is the fruit of thy womb, Jesus.
Holy Mary, Mother of God,
pray for us sinners,
now and at the hour of our death.
Amen.

13.

AMELIA EARHART'S LAST LETTER TO HER HUSBAND READ –

PLEASE KNOW THAT I AM QUITE AWARE OF THE HAZARDS. I WANT TO DO IT BECAUSE I WANT TO DO IT. WOMEN MUST TRY TO DO THINGS AS MEN HAVE TRIED. WHEN THEY FAIL, THEIR FAILURE MUST BE BUT A CHALLENGE TO OTHERS.

Chimera opened her eyes and had to remind herself where she was. Brooklyn. Greenpoint. Arthur. Not in Manhattan anymore. The room was flooded in light from the window and everything inside seemed crisp and white and clean. She rolled over to find a stack of books that stood taller than she currently was from her position on the blow-up mattress on the floor. On top, a hand-written note on the back of a take-out menu read:

Have you ever been real close to something?
Once, I was so close to the sun that I could not
look around it or past it or turn away from it.
It is louder there than you'd think,
a mountain of fire burning.
When the flames embraced me, I fed it.
Happy New Year – Arthur

Sitting up, she realized they were all autobiographies though she failed to recognize more specifically that they were all autobiographies of women. Chimera thumbed to the last pages on a few of the books, smiling. She glanced over to her stack of papers, her manuscript, safe in the corner. Was that a poem? She wasn't sure what it meant exactly—was she the fire? What a dark, fantastic mind.

She got up and opened the bedroom door. Listening for a moment, she heard nothing and saw no movement. Her view was the empty living room, an old TV staring straight at her.

"Hello?" She called out. There was no reply. The Noyes must be gone.

She moved around the house, picking things up and placing them back in their space. The house itself was like a library—it seemed that nearly all wall space that was not occupied by windows was filled with shelves stacked in books or papers. The first floor was the living room, a small yellow kitchen, and her room underneath the stairs. There was a closet off the living room that housed rain slickers, thick sweaters, and boots and shoes—all in varying sizes and colors. Lastly, there was a bathroom that was so small that Chimera could sit on the toilet and still take a shower. The sink was the size of a soup bowl.

Upstairs, Chimera discovered two rooms—one was obviously Arthur's. It held a large bed, a dresser, and a wooden desk. There was a framed black-and-white photo of a woman, maybe in her late twenties, that sat off to the side of the dresser and the rest of the surfaces were covered with loose or bound papers, books and notepads, and strewn writing instruments of every variety. The desk had one drawer that sat right above the lap of whoever sat working there. Chimera tugged at its handles but it wouldn't open. There was something inside there though; she could hear it shift slightly against the wood. Kneeling down, she noticed a brass keyhole. Taking this as a sign to give up, she moved towards the other room. The last room had two small beds and must have been the children's room though it did not have any toys or mess or bright colors that Chimera would expect to see. It was a lot like her room, painted completed white (walls, floor and ceiling) and shelves upon shelves of books punctured by a sole naked window. There were two dressers, both painted white.

Chimera would soon learn that the basement was occupied by an older lady for extra income. As far as Chimera would ever know, she spoke no English. She lived down there in the basement silently like a furnace underneath the rest of them. The first Monday of each month, she would leave her rent in a plain white envelope filled with bills in Arthur's mailbox. Chimera would occasionally see her in the early morning shuffling down Franklin towards the deli by the park. Otherwise, she didn't seem to exist to Chimera.

During the month of January, Chimera quickly resumed her housewife status, except this time she actually had some responsibility as there were two children living with them. Though alien to her, Chimera enjoyed the responsibility. She took the kids to school and daycare in the morning and picked them up at night. She inquired about their days with genuine interest. Of course, she only ever got responses from the girl.

Arthur was a property manager for three buildings in Williamsburg owned by Hasidic Jews. His job responsibilities included collecting the rent checks, dropping off those rent checks to South Williamsburg, and helping show the rooms when they became vacant. Hours were sparse and all over the place. It left Arthur with a lot of free time, most of which he spent in his room behind a closed door. He suffered from an acute agita when he did not devote a certain amount of time to his studies: reading, writing, and thinking. Chimera left Arthur completely alone until he came down the stairs and approached her for conversation. Often this didn't happen until late in the evening.

It only took about two weeks until this became their routine. Silence and creating in the morning, Chimera as a herder of the children at dawn and dusk, and evening full of conversations about art and creation and questions about the point of Life. Sometimes, these conversations would occur in the living room with the dead television staring at them and sometimes it was at The 156 after the kids were asleep, but either way there was usually whiskey involved. Arthur was never really much of a drinker before Chimera and, at first, it felt like he was proving something to her by keeping up with her drink for drink. Quickly, it became an integral part of their routine. It numbed something for both of them.

Sometimes, their words connected—in that,

both of them actually understood what the other was saying. However, inevitably, there were times where Chimera had no idea what Arthur was talking about. She heard the words, understood them individually, but the way he lined them up made them indiscernible to her. Yet, she enjoyed not understanding Arthur in a way that she had not with Delores or her other relationships. She felt a heavy subtext within him and wanted to work through its mystery. She supposed she enjoyed thinking that she was close to solving some complex puzzle.

Excerpts of their conversations were as follows:

1. Arthur: "We make an idol of our Fear and that idol we call G-d." {Chimera knew that wasn't him—those weren't his thoughts—but loved the sentiment.} Recycling words and sentiments, a habit she knew quite well.

2. Chimera: "I can't even think about the Middle East. Sometimes, out of no where, I get this flash of an image—a large bright light with all the protons and neutrons and electrons speeding past taking the corresponding parts of you with them, and it's the most horrifying vision of finality, the wind—the light framed by light, and you

can feel it's heartbeat in Mecca (qiblah, qui blah blah blah). "

3. Arthur: "You know, in language, you have a lexicon and its grammar: the words (a body) and how to use them (it's engine— tiny, red beating heart)."

4. Chimera: "Have you ever seen Paul Auster? [Arthur shakes his head no.] He has a face that looks like it belongs in an old photograph, like he belongs in sepia. This unsmiling, melancholy face—""Austere Auster," Arthur quips and they both laugh at something made funnier by intoxication.

One day, at the 156 with a soccer game on the TVs, Arthur turns to Chimera and looks directly into her eyes. They were talking about the progress of her manuscript, about the appropriate place to stop. He paused and then asked, "Can you being doing a good thing even if it hurts someone else?"

"How do you mean?" Chimera did not know what he could be referencing. How was collecting words hurting her?

"I don't know exactly how to phrase it." He didn't look away. Instead he moved in closer towards her. His wayward eyes still managed to catch hers directly through angles and intensity. He was sweating softly as usual. The liquor was brightening his cheeks. "It's an ethics question I suppose. Would you do something for the greater good even if it meant temporarily hurting someone?"

"Sacrifice the individual to benefit the rest of humanity?"

"Kind of."

"I don't get it. Like a just war?"

"Yes, I suppose. Just answer. I don't know how to describe it any better."

"I don't know," Chimera said. "I guess. You have to do what you think is right. But I don't know if I could kill someone."

"You don't have to kill anyone."

"Ok... well, I don't know. I don't know what you're talking about."

Another routine spawned from lazy Sundays after church. Chimera would meet the Noyes (and/or Numen-Noyes) a block away from Our Lady, half-hiding from and half-wanting to see Delores. They would walk up the stairs to the JMZ and head into the city to spend the afternoon wandering around Chinatown, with the looming buildings of the Financial District framing their red-gold scene (concrete on concrete). There was some comfort in knowing that these grey behemoths were cradled by the sea.

They would make it down to the Financial District eventually where the cobbled streets were slick but empty. Outside the hole where the World

Trade Center stood, there would be throngs of European tourists but in between the taller buildings, closer to the park, there was literally no one (that is to say less than a dozen people) and it would feel like they owned New York. On the East side in particular, with the small older taverns and restaurants dwarfed by the skyline, with pretty street names like Pearl and Liberty and Maiden, there was a pocket of cold, grey solitude that made Manhattan feel like a giant ruin they were exploring. Down there, Arthur let Chimera hold his hand (never fingers intertwined, always palm to palm like a prolonged Catholic answer—*Peace Be With You*) and the kids could run out a little ways in front of them and, for an hour or two, Chimera felt like they were an actual family—they felt like the first family, like Adam and Eve, or maybe it was the last family, taking a Sunday stroll in a dead city (in a dead New York, in a dead world). Sometimes it is difficult to differentiate the first from the last, or to tell where the circle started. It is hard for Chimera to remember all the steps that got her to where they were right now.

Mothers have long lectured their daughters on how your heart can trick you into feeling something very close to love. Men don't seem to have an equivalent experience. And it was true. Chimera felt like she fell in love with everyone she bumped into—*I can convince myself to love anyone.* Le coeur volé. Maybe Love doesn't feel like something specific—maybe it comes and goes—maybe something is good enough or something is better than nothing at all. Maybe it doesn't matter as long as you can make something better. Benefit something outside yourself.

Arthur was undeniably benefiting her; the financial support and the room of her own. So she had to make herself useful to him. They weren't sleeping together or anything vaguely romantic outside of their conversations and the occasional handholding. Since Gabriel, Chimera felt vaguely asexual anyway. So she was his housewife without the wife part—she took care of the children and he made it clear that he expected her to write daily ("Create!"). It was so comfortable for her there that she let any perceived unpleasantries fall under—not a blind but perhaps a silent—eye.

It bugged her for a while—the question of why she felt an attraction, some invisible magnetism, towards Arthur Noyes. The answer she kept coming back to, no matter how unsatisfactory, was that he was just so different from her. It was the same justification she felt with Delores. She did not yet understand him at all. And he was passionate about something larger than himself or the mundane elements of life people become obsessed with (clothes, cars, cash, etc., etc.). This made him more different than anyone else she had ever known. Simply, he was interesting.

And there was the fact that he actually looked

at her. When they were together, he was always looking at her, though often it was in waiting for her to look at him.

Chimera didn't think Arthur was a particularly good artist, and by that Chimera meant he wasn't especially creative or bright or original. She had read a lot of what he had written and it was rambling and so laden with meaning Chimera would never ascertain (if it was there at all). They never seemed to be in any order either, just collections of thoughts circling around into and away from themselves. But he was entertaining and he understood dynamics—and at his very best, he was an excellent collector and identifier of exquisite snippets of humanity (capturing that fleeting feeling of sublimity verbalized by common people, and uncommon people, things said in bars or bedrooms or on sidewalks), like a photographer of words or an archivist of sentiment. He preserved sentences and compiled them into a paper exhibit and his readers (who so far were only Chimera and some Power outside himself) felt the sad commonality we all share. He could speak of those big things—of Love, and Death, and Sex, and Life—without using those words, without establishing dichotomies or assigning cliché symbols. So Chimera supposed he had talent, perhaps because he was so emotive, but more so because he recycled emotion most efficiently and, when she thought of it like that, that's what might have made him the best artist she had ever known.

He had that bravado, that self-assurance that Chimera was pretty sure only men felt. He said so confidently that he was an artist—Definitive—What do you do? I'm an artist, I'm a poet, like he was Bukowski or Hemingway or Hunter S. Thompson. Definitive—The words, heavy as stones, didn't sink into the ground. They built an artifice around the man, and if anything he was a man—sparse, sharp words and, underneath the smell and semen and facial hair, the underlying ebb of passion. A man among men who wasn't afraid of fight or liquor or flight, who legitimately did not give a fuck one way or another what you or anyone else thought of him, who found no fear in vulnerability but, in it, a secret all the more powerful. Chimera supposed if you court Death long enough, you will feel as powerful as G-d and see the romance all around in everything moving past. She had heard him say, or rather drunkenly mumble, "I don't think I can be destroyed. I don't think they can, I don't think they can."

That was the first moment that Chimera felt something could be truly wrong with Arthur. There were things that hinted at it before, obviously. But those moments were covered by drink and denial. That sentence, though. It stuck out to Chimera. Everything can be ruined. Every single thing. Nothing is outside of an End.

In the beginning was the Word, and the Word was with G-d, and the Word was G-d. But before that, presumably, was no Word. No G-d. And after us, presumably, there will be no more words. After we die, there will be no meaning.

Other things began to worry her too as they sunk further into their routine. Chimera, at first, was so focused on Arthur, on maintaining his affections and understanding him, and on drinking, that the children were initially an afterthought. Or a chore. It also didn't help that they were both very distant from Chimera at first. Leery. Silent. Small. Yet, as Chimera grew to feel that they were a unit, maybe even a family in some way, the subtle interactions Chimera continued to witness between Arthur and Mary, and Arthur and Pesach, and Mary and Pesach began to give her increasing concerns.

With Mary, Chimera noticed that she was tight-lipped but selectively verbal and seemingly intelligent. However, Arthur passed her by like she was a shadow. Though other men didn't. Chimera noticed Mary attracting attention from strangers walking down the sidewalk in her striped leggings and she worried that Mary Numen-Noyes was at that magical age—when little girls stop being little girls and suddenly become something to fuck.

When Chimera was eight, her body was

different. It was thinner and smaller. But by the time she was twelve, Chimera distinctly remembers the boys in the grades above her saying she had 'nice tits' and asking her if she had ever stuck various items inside (cucumbers, staplers, whatever was in sight). Mary was around eight or nine years old. She hadn't yet lived an entire decade. Finnegan once told Chimera that every guy, not matter who, wanted to fuck every woman that passed him on the street. Other past, faceless boyfriends had echoed that sentiment more or less, though usually with more tact. And Chimera was noticing men looking at Mary like she was a woman. For the first time in her life, she wanted to protect someone outside of herself. She wanted to wrap Mary up in the house and leave her there safe in that sanctuary until she was old enough to understand all these motives and words and physical movements.

As for Pesach, he remained completely silent like a celibate monk or a blank, gaping void. As the days passed that January, Chimera realized he never said a word or even grunted. He would lift his sad brown eyes to meet yours but his face was the most stolid countenance she had ever seen on a child. Even when he got upset, as children do, his cries were silent, just tears falling across his red cheeks, and a slight trembling that might be imperceptible from across a room. Arthur treated Pesach differently than Mary. While Mary he ignored, Arthur seemed enraptured by Pesach. Holding his shoulders between his two meaty paws and kneeling down to look him straight in the eye, Arthur seemed to speak to Pesach through mental telepathy. Everything passed between their eyes.

Anytime Chimera tried to bring up Mary, Arthur barely showed any interest and often just pretended that nothing was said [he would not respond]. As for Pesach, she had only tried once.

They were at home, on the couch. The children were still up and were silently playing in their room upstairs.

"Arthur." A preface.

He looked up. "Yes?"

"Are you concerned about Pesach?"

He stood up. "What? What do you mean?"

Chimera was taken back by his response and the energy behind it. She looked up at him from her seat. "I just.. I mean that he doesn't speak yet."

"Oh." Arthur sat down again, breathing out in relief. Then, sternly, "No."

They both sat in silence looking at each other. Chimera held a glass to her lips for a moment, thinking.

"I'm not concerned at all. Pesach is a good boy—very healthy boy." Arthur said, the arch of his voice smoothing. "He speaks volumes, but so far it's just to me. And perhaps his sister."

Arthur suddenly seemed very flustered. He spoke the way people do when they're thinking of something outside the conversation. Stilted. Rapidly. Disconnected. "I have a plan. It will fix any problems. Anyway, I have a plan..."

He looked at her again and then, with a quiet intensity, said, "It's not really your concern anyway. You are not his mother."

His voice was clear and bubbled with a deep dissonance.

When Arthur sat back down, his hand landed in the crux of his jeans and her breath held in the crux of her heart.

Chimera lifted the glass again and thought *What am I doing? What should I do? What can I do when I don't understand anything around me?*

Looking down at his feet, Chimera asked, "Can I clip your toenails?"

Arthur face broke into a quick smile and he shook off his slippers, leaning back. Chimera went to fetch a tub to soak his feet and the clippers. It was their most intimate physical act; probably more so than anything she had ever done with Finnegan (though less so than many things she had done with Delores).

14.

FREDERICK DOUGLASS ASKED, "WHY, WHAT DOES THIS MEAN?"

February 1st, 2013. 2 1 2013. 3 33. 3 is a magical number. A good sign. It houses the trinity. It was the 21st of Shevat too. It was also Shabbas. The daily lesson spread out before him –

"Remember you are not the body. Neither are you the animal that pounds within the body, demanding its way in every thing. You are a G-dly soul.

Do not confuse the pain and struggle of the body with the joy and purity of the G-dly soul."

Today was the day. Time for action—everything pointed to this grey and holy day. Six years in the making (5 years and 9 months). Arthur would wait until dusk to start the Pesach seder. He had to cleanse the house. He lit some candles. He sent the girl with Chimera to the city with an impossibly long list of chores. They set out with Chimera's hand tightly grasped around the girl's. Arthur smiled at the back of their heads.

In and out.

Back and forth.

Creation.

Arthur set up a folding table in the living room and spread out a white cloth on top of it. Around the table, he arranged candles on bookshelves and atop the television. He laid out on the table a few key items: a large bowl of salt water, a bottle of whiskey, a knife, three matzot on a white paper plate, a cup, a bundle of papers held together with a taut rubber band like a scroll, and some dish towels. He was preparing for the marking of his 1st born son.

There was also a large silver platter, like one you might serve a turkey on. That was for the boy to lie on. Like a turkey, face up. Or perhaps a lamb that had been led to a slaughter.

"Pesach. Pesach!" Arthur called from the bottom of the stairs.

Pesach's sad face entered the space at the top like a shadow. A slight, dark ghost. Arthur smiled. He saw so much of himself in the boy. *Today's the day.*

"Come down now, my little lamb. It's time for supper."

When Pesach reached the landing, Arthur leaned over to look straight in his face, his arm around Pesach's slight shoulders, and asked, "Do you know why this night is different from all other nights?"

It was time for the transfiguration.

* * *

Shortly after the first of February, Arthur had a dream in which they made love. It was in a bathroom of a brownstone that was his house, but not really his house (because 116 Oak Street in reality was covered in brown shingles). They made love in the bathtub, in the water, surrounded by white walls, the odd, off-white incandescence sweating off the titles. Little 1×1 mirrors opaquely bouncing back their tiny grey bodies in the confusion of love. It looked like a luke-warm struggle, like a larger body enveloping the smaller. Curling into themselves. In the dream, Arthur felt a heat when the belly pressed up against him (a quick breath in deeply to retract that fanny pack of fat). It felt like a slow song, a soft, sad voice. Things like that happen in brownstones in Brooklyn.

This wouldn't end well.

He woke up sweating underneath a thin sheet. Good god. What the hell was that? Was this a sign? Arthur felt the immediate compulsion to make arrangements to get Chimera out of his house. For the first time, Arthur thought of her like a poison or some disease spreading itself internally without Arthur's consent. He didn't need her. He never had. She wasn't a girlfriend. He wanted an audience, silent. Not a mother. Not a wife. Not a parent to help him define the difference between right and wrong. He didn't need someone around who could interrupt the perfect execution of his plan.

She was creeping across borders. It had started when she stopped listening and started asking questions. Now he was dreaming of base pleasures, of baths and breaths and the expansive echo of his body made busy by love. He was disgusted by the tenderness he felt in his dream. It felt real.

At any rate, now he would have to talk to her. They hadn't had one of their conversations in a few days. Arthur stayed upstairs writing and reading and tending to Pesach, who lay ill in Arthur's bed. They had remained cocooned away from the rest of the world together in that bedroom, only really leaving to go to the bathroom. Chimera's face, from the frame of her open door, would follow them as they passed by. Sometimes the girl's face would appear in that frame with Chimera hovering close to her like a black cloud. They had become close, those two, and Arthur couldn't decide if it bothered him or not. He had bigger things on his mind right now. This was a holy movement he was making with each step. It was bigger than those two and bigger than themselves. It was probably the most important to happen in the past 2000 years. He would shut the bathroom door behind them to lock out the unblinking feminine gaze.

From his experience and his studies, Arthur knew that all would be right by the next full moon. They only had to hold out for a few more days, maybe weeks. Then it would be all over and everything would be fixed and Arthur will have created the most important thing since Adam and the garden.

He climbed downstairs. Chimera was already back from having taken the girl to school and Pesach was asleep, curled up like a ball in the middle of Arthur's bed. Chimera was sitting on her blow-up mattress, her knees covered by the thin seashell sheet and a book in her lap. He went to the bathroom first and then paused outside her doorway listening. He couldn't hear anything but the occasional turn of the page.

Arthur moved inside her doorframe and leaned causally against the wood. "What're you up to?"

Chimera looked up surprised. A fear had replaced their easy conviviality. They had realized they didn't know each other at all. It had been all black-outs and babbling up to this point, with the occasional grasping towards finding something more in each other. She gestured with her free hand into her lap. "Reading."

"How has your book been coming along?"

"Which one? The one I'm reading or the one I'm writing?"

"You know what I mean."

Chimera paused and squeezed her lips into a thin line. "How's Pesach?"

Arthur didn't answer at first. So Chimera continued, "... I've been concerned."

"He's ill. But he'll get better."

"Should we take him to the hospital?"

"No. He's fine."

Chimera was silent for a moment. "I'm afraid you're gelding the lily."

Struck by that sentiment, Arthur burst out with a loud, short laugh. How anyone ever understood each other was becoming more and more unfathomable to him.

"What?" Chimera asked, angrily. She obviously didn't think this was funny.

"It's *gilding* the lily. Gelding is..." A pause, two sets of eyes looking right into each other's dark centers in a way that rarely happens in normal conversation but had become something expected between them. A line of connection drawn in a perfect, unerrored filament. "It is something completely different. Never mind. Nothing about it is what you mean."

That was enough for now. Though he was

smiling, Arthur was annoyed. Sometimes that girl seemed smart and, other times, she showed herself to be an idiot like all of the rest of them. Arthur walked away without saying anything. Though she helped with the girl, Chimera was not the willing audience he had thought. The longer they knew each other, the more questions she had and the more he saw she didn't understand. He went upstairs and shut his door. Sitting at his desk, he pulled out a book from a series called Corpus Christianorum. It was entitled "Enarrationes in Psalmos" by Saint Augustine of Hippo. It had Latin on the odd pages and the English translation on the even. He was reading it to make himself feel better. Arthur spent the rest of the day with that text.

The part he was most interested in was where it read—

Caro tua, coniunx tua.

It means *your body is your wife.* Augustine speaks about how at first man existed with these two elements in perfect harmony. But after the Fall, once sin came in, the body and the soul became in constant combat with each other. Your body, a human body, must remain faithful only to itself. Love your body. Keep it pure because it houses your soul. Also, to remember that you have everything you need inside yourself.

His eyes grew tired and his wrist began to strain from his note taking. It was dark again when

Arthur curled up by Pesach. He spooned Pesach like a pearl inside himself. Arthur pressed his lips tenderly to Pesach's head.

All night, that baby cried. His baby cried. Quiet, intangible sadness trembled out of him. His small body emanated a pain Chimera or Arthur or Mary could never share. It was the weight of the responsibility in him—to right all the wrongs his Father saw in this world. He had to carry this weight in silence. Below him, around him, Arthur and Mary slept and Chimera slept even deeper inside some liquor womb. He suffered alone. We all suffer alone.

Bright blades of light had cut that holy night into innumerable parts. Behold the Lamb of G-d, who takes away the sins of this world.

15.

EUGENE O'NEILL JR.'S SUICIDE NOTE READ - *NEVER LET IT BE SAID OF AN O'NEILL THAT HE FAILED TO EMPTY A BOTTLE. AVE ATE VALE.*

Chimera had lasted for years in a depression and, as life dragged on, everything seemed to get worse and worse. It is inevitable—that the longer you live, the more you lose. Ryōshin 両親 (*parentes Aoki*), Delores, and Gabriel—the angel baby. Friends disappearing into their own problems and unhappinesses. But one day something just clicked. It wasn't love from a man or a woman or a friend. It wasn't a sudden fall into wealth or some type of recognition. It was internal and it happened when she was completely alone. It was the epiphany that she needed to do something to make this mess better. She couldn't wallow any longer in this filth.

She woke up on a mid-February morning, her white room almost glowing in the white morning sun, and felt like she was sinking. Her chest was heavy as a stone but her head felt like it was melting away. That morning, before she found the suffering that existed in Arthur's bed, Chimera's thoughts ran out through the fog behind her eyes like a distinct voice from above—*I must make this better while I'm here.* She didn't need anyone to save her if she was the savior and, for the first time in many years, she emerged from the haze.

Though not physically. Her body was severely damaged from a prolonged whiskey bender. She was glued to her bed by sweat and her heart was racing so hard and fast, so uncomfortably, it felt as if it were clawing to get out of her chest. She thought for a moment of calling 911 but fear stopped her (of money, of knowledge, of Arthur). She reached for the bottle near her bed and took a large swallow and waited. She waited to feel something still, but the beating did not subside. It didn't help. It made it worse. Her Heart. Beat.

To stave off panic, she lay completely still and tried to distract herself from the thrashing inside her chest. So she spoke to herselves. *What am I doing to myself? Why have I allowed myself to live like this? Where am I? Show me, inside the lines.*

Eventually she managed to stand up from her mattress and slowly hobble to the kitchen. She was drenched by the time she reached the sink and filled up an empty plastic milk carton with water from the kitchen sink. She drank as much as she could and then replaced it until the jug was brimming again. Her heart screamed, throwing itself violently in giant, arrhythmic shudders against her ribcage. *I'm going to die*, she told herself. She made the trip back to her mattress, clutching walls and countertops so not to faint. She chugged water from her gallon while trying to move as little as possible, her body prostrate. Her stomach bulged from everything she had consumed, brimming with a macabre life. G-d, her heart, her heart. It clicked. *Never again.* She repeated this sentence at least a hundred times, trying to stay calm, closing her eyes. Every once in a while, she said silently to the room—*I'm sorry.*

It was well into the next day before she felt the beating in her chest subside. She got up for her mattress to remove the wet sheets. Seashells touched by the lip of the sea. She went to the closet-like bathroom and sat on the toilet for a long time. Her legs tingled with sleep. Eventually she got up and filled her jug with more rusty water from the bathroom sink and returned to her naked mattress. *Never again*, she repeated to herself. Like tearing holes in a beautiful face, this drinking was pointlessly destructive. It was close to killing her. What was the point? She was letting sadness kill her. Other people's sadness. It can't be mine if I don't want it.

"I will never let this happen again," she said out loud. "I will never let secret sadnesses weigh me down into the earth again." No one was there but everyone already knew.

There was a lot of bad there—so much, so pervasive that it became meaningless. But when good comes in, it enters through both chance and choice. Luck and the decision to accept that luck.

It was Tuesday night and the first time in five days that Arthur left Pesach's side. He was going to his group therapy with Delores in the basement of a church in Bushwick. It was a support group for people who had tried to kill themselves. In essence, it was a room of would-be ghosts. Like all rooms.

A room of people trying to understand why they should keep living.

Chimera left her mattress and opened her door beneath the stairs. In the living room, Mary sat silently. Who knows how long she had been by herself. The old TV was on and a pile of papers held together by a yellow clip was on her lap. The pages were filled with the words of the dead. Final, important, lovesick sentiments that belonged to a litany of strangers and, besides the title, not one word of her own. All of it radiated a fear that Chimera had long lived within. Borrowed words. Lines on paper. Chimera kept reading and rereading for years and years, looking for new meaning.

"What are you doing?" Chimera asked.

"Someone should check on brother." Mary said quietly, her face still turned towards the papers in her lap.

Chimera had been afraid of going up there, of what she may find in Arthur's room. She glanced up the stairs and saw a soft light emanating from down the hall. "Ok. Is he ok?"

Mary looked up at Chimera. "No." She said bluntly. "No, he is not. Someone has to help him."

Chimera looked up the stairwell and saw a distant light coming from the master bedroom. She moved up the stairs quietly, listening for anything that might warn her. Part of her kept seeing Arthur's head moving out of the room, stiff and sudden, accusingly, though she knew he wasn't [t]here. She felt her heart beat stronger inside her chest and the blood pressing against her wrists and temples. Why was she scared? Of a little boy no less? Or was it of an invisible presence? What it was to know.

The boy was curled into a circle in the middle of Arthur's bed. He looked infinitesimal compared to everything around him. But, from deep inside him, he generated a heat that Chimera could feel the moment she pushed the door fully open. As she edged closer, Chimera could see that the child was covered in sweat. She placed her hand on his shoulder and he shuddered, but turned his bright, wet face towards her. A lineless face, pure white like an orb, still managed to convey that this body was miserable. Chimera went to remove his pajama top but the boy stiffened against it, terrified.

"Aren't you hot?" Chimera asked, for no particular reason. She knew there wouldn't be a response. This boy was kept from any interactions, a prize hidden away in Arthur's things for only Arthur to look at and play with. Pesach sank back into his circle and squeezed down into himself. Chimera did not touch him again; instead she opened the window at the head of the bed two or three inches. It was February and the wind struck the room suddenly. They both could feel it snake in and dissipate across the room.

The next few moments consisted of Chimera standing silently over Pesach (*Stabat Mater*) trying to read the situation. The boy moved subtly but constantly, like he was at odds within himself. Like he was trying to purge something from deep inside himself. Something bad was happening here. Chimera knew she was staring at a child in terrible pain. But he was mute. She couldn't communicate with him. How can she ask him what is wrong? Did he understand or was he just ignoring her? *How can I help you when I don't know what's wrong and you won't tell me?* Though she felt helpless, she knew that she couldn't just stand there and watch him suffer any longer. They could swim in all the pain that had leaked out from them in the past few nights.

Chimera sat on the edge of the bed, and stroked the sheets by the little boy. She whispered, "What's wrong, Gabriel? Why won't you tell me?"

She heard a noise behind her. Turning around, Chimera saw Mary standing in the shadows of the hallway, bawling so hard that it engulfed her whole body.

"Mary."

"I'm scared!" She cried.

"I know, me too." Chimera went to move towards her but Mary sunk back.

"*You*—You are scaring me."

Chimera started crying too. As she turned her head from one child to the other, she noticed a jar sitting on Arthur's cluttered desk. It held a yellowish water and a small white mass with a thick rubber band twisted around its base. She moved closer, squinting, her hand at her mouth. Flecks of white and yellow hung as if suspended like an aurora around the mass. Whatever it was, pickled inside that jar, Chimera could tell it used to be alive.

At that moment, Chimera realized it was done.

Arthur had been collecting them. Preserving them as they had been when he had found them. In alcohol, in brine. He made it so that they served no purpose outside of him. She had to leave this house. Now. Before everyone in this godforsaken town swallowed her completely whole.

"Pack your bags." Chimera said to Mary. "Pack Pesach a bag. Of clothes—we don't need anything else. No. Pack a small bag of food too. We're getting out of here."

"Where are we going?" Mary was still crying and the words came out hard, staccato.

Chimera was already at the bottom of the stairwell and moving quickly but she called behind her, "A better place. It will be better. I will be right back. Don't be scared. I'll be right back. And it will be better." And then she exited the front door.

"That's what they always say." Mary cried to the door.

Chimera walked through the lightly dusted fringe of the Northern Brooklyn shoreline. She curved around Greenpoint, shooting across the park into Williamsburg, and then moved into Bushwick. She felt like she moved quickly but, in reality, it took her over a half hour in the cold night to reach the church. It was 9 o'clock when she got there. The crowd was dispersing but Arthur was nowhere to be seen. Chimera didn't even see Delores' shocked face as she moved inside and down the stairs, into the basement of Our Lady.

Down there, Chimera found him, all alone and in the corner underneath a long fluorescent light. The forward momentum that she had gained along the way suddenly ceased, and she felt pushed back by his presence. Slowed or subdued.

Chimera approached him cautiously and finally sat across from him. He hadn't looked over at her in her entire trip across the basement floor. She hadn't planned on what to say when she got there; she had just felt an innate compulsion to confront him. To make him answer for himself, when he seems one way but turns out to be something else. Instead of something eloquent, she simply said, "I'm leaving."

"I'm not surprised." Arthur didn't move. It was true—he didn't seem surprised or upset. It was all very placid. He was hunched over so that his shoulders seemed to almost reach his knees.

Chimera shook her head, staring down at him. "Well. Why?"

"Why what?"

She wasn't sure. "Why don't you care about anyone but yourself?"

He shook his head. "Nothing has ever been about you. And if you thought so, you've been confused."

"Then what I am doing here? Why did you bring me to Greenpoint?"

"A divine love made me. Everything I do or have ever done has been for my children."

Chimera burst into tears. "Why don't you love me?" She was practically screaming. She hadn't stopped to ask herself why she felt like she needed him to. It just felt like it (love, his love) was owed to her.

There wasn't a pause. "I am the head and you are the body surrounding the heart. There will invariably be distance between us as I lead you around this life."

Arthur shifted, turning towards her—the split vision caught her in between his eyes. He looked at her slack-jawed, gaping lips, and furrowed, black eyes. He could tell she didn't look satisfied with that answer. He breathed out heavily.

"Think about when you could still wrap your mouth around these words, meaning allusive and time an as-of-yet unknown tyrant. Before mediocrity and loneliness and phobias and accidents, before death, before tears solidified behind every blink, before definition became a never-ending burden instead of a gift. Before there was this ever-present anxiety lining the skin from inside, pink dotted with awful red, a dappled nightmare, the corpse slowly pressing out, everything moving towards light and eventually the ugly organ of my heart will touch the earth, a thousand tiny breasts slick with mucus will dance upon it and then the worms can feast on something I've tried so hard to protect. To protect but to also share. And it has its share of cracks. I am not perfect."

The purple desk-chair held shadows where it had once embraced the human frame and Chimera leaned back, placing the least known parts of her exterior into its grainy cuddle.

Everything was eerily alive, some pulsating throughout. The source seemed to radiate from the large wooden crucifix on the wall that held up the melancholy savior, blood-paint in tiny rivulets from his man-made punctures and the thick glaze coating illuminated the statue, mimicking the impossible ideal of a corporeal Christ by any glint of light which gave way to illusions of sweat and tears, a fallible man. So Jesus himself sat square above Arthur, a pinnacle the whole room ached towards, all energy trying to reach the old grey wood of Jesus' perch. If the events had not transpired this past week, both Pesach and Chimera sweating out invisible demons and Arthur's looming, sudden silence that fell over 116 Oak (all words held inside one small body—made ill with those words and sentiments), Chimera would have felt very out of place. She would have been nervous.

At that moment, a light blinked out and a shadow fell on Arthur's shoulder from the crucifix and it blended with him, so that it was impossible to tell where the two touched, overlapped. Just amorphous black, the inescapable shadows that permeated that night.

Everything was one.

She felt like spitting.

"People love symmetry—it's irrational. A perfection of balance." Chimera replied (a closer examination would reveal her jagged outline, red white blazed candy stripes).

And, then, she left.

"What?" Arthur asked the empty room.

Chimera moved through the light snow, so fast it felt like swimming. She was moving towards Mary and Pesach. She was going to move them past this moment in their lives. Sober, she could see past Arthur. Outside him. She had accomplished her mission of having given Arthur her final word. Now she had to rectify the wrongs he had afflicted on these children; through too much love or not enough.

Maybe Gabriel was a message. With different choices, Chimera could have been anywhere in the world right now. But every step had led her here—everything had happened for a reason, every horrible thing held a specific purpose.

What could it be? Will he say it was a fugue? (she hummed a little ditty against the traffic until some obscure climax) Maybe his entire life had been an unconscious movement—a sad, sweeping figure-8 bumping into the swell of other cells, refracted like a mosh-pit of light, struggling flailingly like sperm in a Petri dish, all turning together into themselves (Themself? singular) like the inside of a conch-shell, strands of DNA circling into a golden number somewhere outside zero and one.

Maybe he *was* G-d. Or maybe he was just some sad number is an infinite sea of numbers struggling to create a pattern, manipulate the numbers around him to an [specific] order that [actually] had some meaning.

Is that such a bad thing? Is there such a bad thing?

Later, days from that moment, there would be many conversations between people who were strangers to the children, to Arthur, and to Chimera. They all went something close to this—

"How can a child slip through the cracks?"

"What do you mean—what child doesn't? Have you ever met a happy adult?"

"But this is egregious!"

"Everything's relative."

* * *

When Chimera and Mary walked around Brooklyn on the evening of the first of February, set out with a heavy list of chores and with secret magic happening back at home unbeknownst to them, they confided in each other:

Sometimes when she lies down at night to go to sleep, she can feel the Earth moving. It begins as barely perceptible circumambulations and, as sleep sets in, they grow faster and faster. Soon, if she squeezes her eyes together, she can feel the air flying through her hair and her nightgown shifting violently due to the great tempestuous exhalation of the Earth below her. One night she knows Earth will secretively push her towards the white pockets of clouds hidden in the shadows of the black night sky. She will hide all night among the stars until the sun appears and she evaporates.

She often tries to stifle her sobs as the room spins faster and faster around her. The emotions are layered too high, the feelings too dense to move through. It feels like a fog inside behind her eyes, just thickly concentrated vapor.

Chimera/Mary told her that she knows exactly what she's talking about.

* * *

It took Chimera a while to understand that every man is the myth he creates for himself. Each takes truth and fallacy in varying amounts but makes it seem like it is not for anyone else to determine which parts are which. To be with a man is to live within their fiction. Chimera got lost in all of Arthur's words, drunk on each glyph. It was always easy for Chimera to confuse infatuation with some deeper. He had every black mark arranged in such a way that Chimera thought it spread out like a path but, in reality, they circled into a darkening cage.

She reached 116 Oak Street but didn't ascend

the four short steps to Arthur's front door. Instead, she knocked on the door to the basement apartment and the old woman who lived inside. After a few moments of no answer, Chimera banged louder. Sharp, chaotic hits that scrapped the skin off of her knuckles. The door finally opened, and in it, stood a small body, thick but frail, leaning across the frame. Chimera had no idea what the woman said but she did not seem happy.

"Rent." Chimera said.

The lady looked confused. Her face seemed to fold into itself. Soft skin and lines on lines. Her answer was sharp but unintelligible.

"I need your rent money now. Money. Now." Chimera stood with her hand out, flat like a white medallion in the dark.

The woman argued with Chimera and they both yelled at each other in words neither understood. Chimera was getting nasty, swearing at her and near screaming. She was terrified that Arthur might be coming up behind her at any moment. The woman finally slammed her door but Chimera didn't move. She just stood at the door, holding her bleeding hand and letting the tears stream down her face.

Among everything else, Chimera had a fleeting thought of Gabriel. She then realized that you can mend a broken body but you can't revive a part of you once it's dead. A bone, though weakened, will heal, a scrape will dry, but you can't remove something from a body and expect it to grow back. Once something rots inside, you've been poisoned (Chimera's liver, her brain, Pesach's whole body as a small shivering dot—they form a triangle in a body with an axle at the heart). She needed money now to save that child upstairs on the big bed in Arthur's room and to save that girl that no one but strangers noticed. Without it, the three of them would be outside of Port Authority like feral dogs.

The door opened again and Chimera expected to see the woman with a broom to sweep her off the tiny, concrete porch. Instead, the old lady reached out her hand and dropped into Chimera's dumb palm a ten and two fives. A few words muttered angrily from her mouth and she shut the door again. If Chimera had paused to think about what it was that woman said, she would have guessed, based on their exchange and the affect in which they were expressed, that it was something along the lines of "Go fuck yourself". In reality, it was something foreign but closer to "God bless you."

Chimera raced upstairs and found the children waiting in the living room, watching the large, old television. Two backpacks sat on the floor beside them. Pesach was still in his pajamas and looked exhausted. Beside him, his sister seemed lost. *Mary, where was she?*

Lost among a sea of dicks. Just like me. Chimera answered herself. But it would be different for

Mary than it had been for Chimera. Chimera reached around her and held Mary close. "Good girl. We gotta get out of here."

Movement was crucial. They needed to move past this before anything could be fixed. Through eyelashes laced with a garland of tears, she moved the children towards their coats and the door. They started out, their little exodus, but Chimera stopped suddenly on her heels. "Wait!"

She disappeared for a moment inside and then returned front door with the jumble of her manuscript in her hands. She had tied the papers together with a rubber band she found in the kitchen.

She had always thought about leaving the city in a romantic gesture, with the scene sprawled like the last few frames of Gone with The Wind. The sky would be stained a reddish-purple, with golden brown puffs strewn throughout its eternity. A dying fire. Instead it was black and, with Pesach cradled in her arms and Mary at her elbow, they moved further and further into it. Brooklyn's dissonance vibrated against the back of their necks as they turned to the water.

I feel like I was just born. I am so vaguely aware of the passage of time—it feels like a day between the sun and the snow.

The G, then the J, brought them to the offices of an illegal Chinatown bus company and there she bought three tickets to Philadelphia using three crumbled bills donated by a complete stranger. Chimera would never recognize it but she had made it through life based on the kindness of strangers. Some might call it luck. They would escape to freedom through the slow-moving Holland Tunnel in the heart of a Greyhound.

16.

"I THOUGHT I DID FOR THE BEST. USELESS! USELESS!" SAID JOHN WILKES BOOTH

A woman leads man to complete ruin.

Who would have guessed it?

What in the Hell was he thinking? Arthur had deviated from the trinity, his trio—he had wanted to have a disciple to help him carry out this glorious plan. A woman should have made him more legitimate, in his mind, according to everything he'd ever known. But he had falsely seen something important in this specific woman—the want to learn, the desire to create something better (something that didn't already exist), and the need for love.

Out loud, he said, "I thought she was beautiful but it was only because I felt like she loved me."

Arthur knew that inside him existed a boundless mercy, but that morning, with the discovery of his empty bed, Arthur pulsated with a wrath he had never known. There were a thousand signs to warn him but his vanity had made him blind.

Cut out my eyes to spite my face.

Smite my eyes.

By Gloucester's eye...

The very last word in the New Testament is (not surprisingly) *AMEN*. And indeed Amen acts like a sigh, a period. A finality. A-men [single/plural].

Revelation 22:21 –

> The grace of our Lord Jesus Christ
> be with you all. AMEN.

But in the Old Testament—the book that spawned everything else—maybe more aptly called the Original Testament—the very last word is *CURSE*.

Malachi 4:6 –

> And he shall turn the heart
> of the fathers to the children,
> and the heart of the children to their fathers,
> lest I come and smite the earth with a CURSE.

A blessing and a threat. It made Arthur think about how love can grow out, violently, from fear and pain. Arthur began to cry again, thinking of the fact that he would not be able to protect Pesach from other's interpretations. From the meaning others found.

When he had gotten home that night, nothing really seemed askew. The house sat quiet and everything seemed to be in its place. Arthur had sat in the living room sipping on the rest of the leftover whiskey from his seder with Pesach. He voided out in front of passing images on the TV screen. Chimera's presence, the heat that she radiated—Arthur could feel it missing from the room underneath the stairs. But he didn't feel the missing presence of Pesach, which is peculiar, since Arthur was in him as much as he was inside Arthur. Everything felt normal, if not slightly cold. February's chill had cloaked their escape. He passed out there, without checking on anyone, bathed in the television's glare.

When he discovered his empty bed the next morning, his head heavy with a hangover and his heart beating wildly in his chest, Arthur knelt down at the base of his bed and sobbed. He had suffered greatly and now he regretted so much. Brutal truth, brutal—a sea of never-known mikvahs that he could never traverse. Alone.

Quod fuimus, estis; quod sumus, vos eritis.

By removing the root of all evil in tHis world, Arthur had created in Pesach an Elysian Field—a tangible paradise. He'd only have to live in a duality: head and heart. Nothing for Arthur's son would be mitigated by longings of the flesh. In essence, Arthur had created a direct line between the body and the soul. A purer body with less tainted meat (just like the pigs; sweet, sweet meat). Pesach Numen-Noyes would be a man without sex, a man who could focus on a higher creation—something his Father could never do. All his Father could do was create an opportunity for him and protect him from evil. It came in many forms: in men, in women, in dancing and bathrooms and books, in dreams and daylight, in the signs everywhere. In his Mothers. And though this woman had stolen them, this was Arthur's ultimate and ever-lasting protection.

With Pesach gone, creation suddenly felt banal. Arthur had spent his life trying to understand what was being said. The rough words, wrought from those large brown hands, from Father's mouth. But the more he learned, the further he got lost. English as an amalgam of bastardized German and some romance. All these texts were then rooted where Latin and Greek and Hebrew collide, babel babble babble—*Gloria Patri, et Filio, et Spiritui Sancto. Sicut erat in principio, et nunc, et semper, et in sæcula sæculorum. Amen.* It always came back—it circled back around again and again.

It took Arthur a long time before he had decided what to do. It hit him after an entire life-time (four decades) of experiences and learning and random circumstance that had landed him in a specific place at a specific moment with a very specific chemistry whirling through his bloodstream; a rash, quiet epiphany stung like an electric shock inside. He was masturbating when an image of the pigs, a memory from the farm, crossed whatever blurred path composed his consciousness.

The night after Father died, Arthur somehow ended up in bedroom Father shared with Annabelle Leigh. It was the same room that Father had shared with his first Mother. Annabelle was seated on the bed, her legs covered by a blue and white quilt. A light shone outward in a yellow pool from the nightstand beside her. Her hands moved fluidly above her lap. She was sewing flowers onto napkin. Father's presence still seemed heavy in that house. Arthur could feel its invisible magnetism from his own room downstairs. Arthur opened the door without a knock and Annabelle looked up at Arthur standing there without surprise.

"What do you want?"

Arthur strode across the floorboards with the gait of confidence, something he had never experienced before and something Annabelle had never seen. With both of his hands, he pulled back her red curls—too rough—and, at the moment, she felt something inside her shatter. She let out a formless protest and he pressed his lips against her roughly. He pressed his face against hers, moving it slowly side to side and waited for a moment to feel anything. But nothing came. Finally, he stood up and looked down at her without saying a word, just looming like a large, grey stone.

The window needs to open; I want to feel the cold.

Arthur turned on his heels and moved to leave.

"Arthur!" Annabelle shouted, like a mother to a son in trouble.

He had made it to the door but had to turn back around.

She planted her hands firmly in her lap. "You know, in this life there are only serpents and seraphim." Arthur's expression remained its classic phlegmatic form but he began to sweat. She continued, with her thin white finger pointed out at him accusingly. "And you, Arthur Noyes, you are a snake on his belly. Out ruining this garden. There is something wrong pitted deep inside you and you reek of sin incarnate. Always have."

Arthur shook his head and responded, "A divine love made me."

She shook her head in disagreement. "You need to leave after his funeral. And I don't want you to ever come back."

He never did, though there was a part of him never left. He carried the farm and their memories inside everywhere he went. Now he was here. Standing on the edge of the East River, twenty-four years later, looking at the jeweled mountain of Manhattan looming in the distance. Most of Brooklyn's waterfront, at least the side that faced its master, was abandoned, lined with old factories and fenced off 'beaches'. Arthur had crawled underneath the rod iron fence like a rat and was pacing the rocky shore in the dark. He had spent the majority of the day curled up in his bed, lying around the memory of the most important part of his life. He could still feel its presence there. Along the shoreline, he saw something moving closer to him from a distance away. It was a small round body becoming more distinct by space. It was nearly by his side before Arthur could tell it was a stray dog. The animal brushed against Arthur in a content supplication but Arthur could not stifle his initial reaction, which was to kick it in its side. "Get the Hell out of here!" Arthur knew from every story he had ever read that when a dog shows up, the protagonist is in a sorry state. The dog disappeared back into the night and Arthur moved further down the jagged outline of Brooklyn's furthest reach.

He was about twenty-four years away from that exact moment of kissing his step-mother. It was the first and last time he ever tried to physically express love to a woman. It was not successful. Yet still, Arthur had managed to have that woman's child's child—someone who was and always would be a stranger to her no matter their ultimate connections—and, with that, they were family. With this boy, Arthur had tried to create the perfect human being. The perfect man, rather. Semantics. Family.

A great chasm had been set in place and it was not of Chimera's making. Something greater put it there, between Arthur and Pesach, a great roaring river. Though his child was an unknown distance away from his Father, Arthur still held a part of him in his rough white hands. What would happen to that perfect boy next? How would Arthur be reunited with this prodigal son? Arthur was still an unknown amount of time away from unknown events.

Calling the police had never crossed Arthur's mind. He thought of them as a group, as a single entity, prone to misunderstanding and violent outbursts. Arthur had never trusted that group. He had read that the crowd is untruth. That shape-shifting girl with her black magic eyes would easily evade them. He also didn't have any legal papers for the boy. He had taken him from Camden without a struggle. No one had known those children existed; they were disposable to everyone except for Arthur. But Margaret, if she was still alive, had the legal rights to them. In the eyes of the law, Arthur himself was a stranger who had stolen them. Everything is up to interpretation. Besides, what would those men think, with what little they know?

All Arthur had to cling to was faith in the idea that they would inevitably be united. He just had to patiently wait at their home, for a sign, for the boy to return when he was able. They had important plans to carry out. The boy knew that. Arthur had looked many times into his blank, sad eyes and told him that they needed each other. Each time, Arthur believed he saw understanding. So all Arthur Noyes could do was wait and mourn these lost years and pray. Count time by the power of three.

"Pray for me," he said aloud, speaking to no one, as usual. His own prayers seamed together, words on words on words on words, until it became a conversation with himself—a question asked, and an answer given. In the dim moonlight and the black and grey soft-shifting shapes of the water rocking beside him, Arthur raised the part of Pesach he still had. Pesach lay in his palm as a white and red emblem and Arthur raised it above the outline of the world like a dead balloon. He stood higher than everything else. Unlike Father's fingers, Arthur could carry Pesach—the root of Pesach—and keep them safe from nonexistence until they were together again.

PESACH—a scream neither internal or external—I AM HERE, YOU ARE SAFE. I AM YOUR FATHER AND YOU ARE MY SON. WE ARE ONE. TOGETHER OR APART. Only the water responded, soft claps and the sound of it swallowing something into its depths forever.

Can you say a fractal when it contains many

fractals?
In infinity, how is there space for more than one
thing?
Or nothing?

As he stood up from scrambling back underneath the iron fence, Arthur began to hum softly a song that abated his tears.

"We'll meet again, some sunny day—"

EPILOGUE

PRESSING HIS HAND TO HIS HEART, SILVIO PELLICO SAID, *"HERE MY GOD IS."*

I'm here again. I only show up for the beginnings and the ends. Just like a real Father. Just like a good Father does. I don't care for the messy in-betweens. I just wanted to let you know that Chimera Aoki and the siblings Numen-Noyes, Mary and Pesach, have made it out of the tunnel and have reached Elizabeth, New Jersey.

* * *

The dark opened up in front of her like a book sat on its spine, a black forever reverberating silence. *I'm scared; I'm scared.* Chimera could feel the new tears starting to well up behind her eyes and the pressure pushing down. She breathed out, one long calming push. The black nothingness of eternity opened in front of her like the ubiquitous arms of a stranger. She breathed out again. A pause, a letting-go. The aching silence. She breathed in.

And she embraced it.

Arthur was not an educated person, but he was a very intelligent person. If she had known the details, Chimera would have lamented his childhood and its effect of his psyche—the prevailing personal catastrophes that ensued as a result of this catalyst. Forty years ago, the incendiary agent that sparked this whole mess was a book, a very old book. The mediating agent, the conduit, *con-do-it,* was his father who read this book, who believed its words, who found meaning within (and then without) this object. He found comfort in all of the voices throughout history that spoke (screamed) through this book; he listened to their rules and learned their lessons. He, like most other men throughout history who had, through luck, procreated, passed his thoughts to his son so he could pass it down to his sons and their sons. Arthur grew up confined to that book. That book had the last word. Through its characters and their trials, Arthur survived his trials and lived his life. Not within the library he had built around himself. Instead, Arthur lived within a single book—within itself, its eternity of meanings, still confined and limited. Its own universe, both ever expansive and ultimately constrained. Can infinity live within a box—can a life be lived within a lifetime? Tanakh. Turbulent doesn't begin to describe... a Mandelbrot Set—

All in all, Death was a cataclysm—bright speeding lights and a noise so loud it sounded like nothing at all. A circling vortex towards the bottom. The inertia of the bus crash, the body crumpling into glass and steel, momentum spilling forward, her mind in and out of the blackness of itself. It was unstoppable and she could not help it or anything anymore. Through her headphones, Bruce Springsteen was singing to her about Atlantic City. The children were sleeping, ever sleeping. The pages of her manuscript billowed out around her, unordered words made meaningless again, but surrounded her in a quiet beauty like new snowflakes. The rain touched them all. Chimera would die, Mary and Pesach would die—they all died without coming any closer to meaning (to understanding any of it—at all).

What had we become? We both had thrown something away—we both made decisions that changed the lives of others. What made us different? Were we ever going to get where we are going?

He had seen us as swine in his life, but there was the fact that though he owned the farm, we had, for a while, kept coming back to the barn. Valued by our flesh, we were malleable and replaceable. The confusion of love was stuck in the slop and mud and shit, and we, Mary and Pesach and I, we were up to our ankles in it, fenced in by its electricity and the shadowy expanse of the world beyond it.

Out behind the round bales, the coyotes ("ki-oates") feast on the carcasses of dead kittens and, even in New Jersey, it smells somewhat like an early Spring. Rot and salt of the sea.

Like a death of sorts.

BIBLIOGRAPHY

Le Comte, Edward, ed. *Dictionary of Last Words.* New York: Philosophical Library, 1955. Print.

Rich, Adrienne. *Of Woman Born: Motherhood as Experience and Institution.* New York: W.W. Norton, 1995. Print.

Swiontkowski, Gale. *Imagining Incest: Sexton, Plath, Rich, and Olds on Life with Daddy.* London: Associated Press, 2003. Print.

ABOUT THE AUTHOR

Jesi Bender is an artist living in Upstate New York, where she lives with her husband and beautiful daughter. She is also a librarian and the head of KERNPUNKT Press, a home to experimental writing. Her work has appeared *Split Lip*, *Lunch Ticket*, and *Paper Darts*, among others. www.jesibender.com

ABOUT THE PUBLISHER

Whisk(e)y Tit is committed to restoring degradation and degeneracy to the literary arts. We work with authors who are unwilling to sacrifice intellectual rigor, unrelenting playfulness, and visual beauty in our literary pursuits, often leading to texts that would otherwise be abandoned in today's largely homogenized literary landscape. In a world governed by idiocy, our commitment to these principles is an act of civil service and civil disobedience alike.